THEY CALL HER
FREGONA
A BORDER KID'S POEMS

DAVID BOWLES

Kokila

Awards and praise for
THEY CALL ME GÜERO
by David Bowles

2018 Texas Institute of Letters Jean Flynn Award
for Best Middle Grade Book

2018 *School Library Journal* Best Book selection, Middle Grade

2018 *Shelf Awareness* Best Children's & Teen Books
of the Year selection, Middle Grade

2019 Pura Belpré Honor Book

2019 Walter Dean Myers Honor Book for
Outstanding Children's Literature

2019 Claudia Lewis Award for Excellence in Poetry

2019 Tomás Rivera Mexican American Children's Book Award

2019 ALSC Notable Children's Books selection

2019 NCTE Notable Verse Novels selection

2019 Américas Award, Commended Title

2019 White Raven selection

2019 Whippoorwill Book Award for Rural YA Literature

2019 Skipping Stones Book Award

2019 Americas Society / Council of the Americas Favorites selection

2020–2021 Texas Bluebonnet List selection

2020–2021 Nominee for the South Carolina Children's Book Award

★ "Vibrant and unforgettable, this is a must-have for all middle grade collections." —*School Library Journal*, starred review

★ "A richly rewarding tour through many borderlands, including adolescence itself, and a defiant celebration of identity." —*Publishers Weekly*, starred review

★ "*They Call Me Güero* makes itself accessible to all readers, without ever moving away from celebrating and directly addressing Spanish-speaking children." —Siân Gaetano, children's and YA editor, *Shelf Awareness*, starred review

"Güero's voice brims with humor, wit, and bits of slang, and a diverse cast of characters offers hints of other cultures. . . . A valuable, too-brief look at the borderlands." —*Kirkus Reviews*

"A welcome contribution to the bildungsroman corpus of Chicana/o literature." —Lettycia Terrones, *The Horn Book*

"While Bowles includes heavy themes of immigration, the sting of racism toward Güero, so called for his pale skin, and the ever-present psychological awareness of being a border kid, lighter moments prevail: the market, music lessons, the best buds' bookworm squad, and family celebrations." —Américas Award, Commended Title

"This slim poetry collection becomes more relevant with each passing day." —Barbara Moon, *Reading Style*

"I love this book!" —Margarita Engle, 2017–2019 National Young People's Poet Laureate

"A masterful novel-in-poems rooted in generations of culture, geography, and story." —Sylvia Vardell & Janet Wong, creators of The Poetry Friday Anthology series

"Bowles has added an important text to borderland writing that would have made the great Gloria Anzaldúa proud. This is a collection that resonates with readers, and that given the current political landscape, demands to be read." —*PANK*

Kokila
An imprint of Penguin Random House LLC, New York

First published in the United States of America by Kokila,
an imprint of Penguin Random House LLC, 2022

Copyright © 2022 by David Bowles

Grateful acknowledgment is made for permission to reprint lines from the song "Mi Fantasía" written by Enrique Negrete Rincón. Published by Tn Ediciones Musicales. Copyright secured.
Used by permission. All rights reserved.

Kokila & colophon are registered trademarks of Penguin Random House LLC.

Visit us online at penguinrandomhouse.com.

Library of Congress Cataloging-in-Publication Data is available.

Manufactured in Canada

ISBN 9780593462577

10 9 8 7 6 5 4 3 2 1
FRI

Design by Jasmin Rubero
Text set in Hypatia Sans Pro

They Call Her Fregona is available in Spanish in paperback
from Penguin Random House Grupo Editorial.

To all the brilliant young fregonas in Eagle Pass who first insisted I write this book.

You were right. Joanna's story needed to be told.

Thank you.

TABLE OF CONTENTS

Thump.
Thump.
My dizzy heart kept swinging
between Heaven and Earth—
it was my first love.

—from "The Physics of Love"
by Kim In-yook

WINTER PROLOGUE

FESTIVE BARBECUE

Christmas Eve—a perfect excuse
to throw meat on the grill.
With tíos and primos, I crowd close
to Dad, watching the sizzle.
Smiles and warmth shine on our faces—
frigid wind rises at our backs.

BORDER SNOW

Evening becomes dark night,
unusually hushed and cold.
Our house stands, strung
with lights, the glowing heart
of our ruby-red orchard.

Festivities have wound down;
my cousins sprawl asleep
on sofas and floor, their parents
nodding off as *Miracle on 34th Street*
drones quiet and ever-magic.

I'm sitting in the gloom of my room,
staring at her texts on my phone.
The door opens with a slow groan.
"Güero," my dad whispers.
"You awake? Come on, son."

I wipe a tear from my cheek
before he switches on the light.
It's almost midnight, Christmas Eve.
"Wait, Dad," I say, filled with worry.
"What's up? Everything okay?"

"Shh. Trust me. Come outside to see
a gift like none you've ever received:
pure joy, scattered down from the sky."
Though his tone is weird, I follow him
down the hall, out the back door—

the world has been dusted white.
Christmas snow. Impossible.
"A hundred years since it's happened,"
Dad says, taking crunching steps,
face glowing with awed delight.

A soft kiss. Snowflakes drift down
like icy stars that speck the black.
Fragments of magic, divine dust,
blessings shaken out upon my head
by God Himself. I pull out my cell.

She answers, voice creaky with sleep.
"Look outside, Joanna," I tell her.
She gasps. "¡Está nevando, Güero!"
"Merry Christmas, bae. I miss you."
"Me too. So much. Te hablo mañana."

I look at my dad. He nods at the weight
of her absence. We stand together,
silent for a moment, the house holy
in its robe of snow, the trees pale
sentinels beneath the clouds.

Then we tumble back onto the dazzling
blanket pulled loose over crabgrass,
and for a moment we are angels,
laughing and innocent as we spread
our silver wings upon the earth.

MY JOURNAL

After we wake everyone up,
after the midnight snowball battle,
after the little snow people have turned
the huercos' bare palms bright red—
Mom makes a pot of chocolate.

With my steaming mug
trailing the scent of cinnamon and almonds,
I head back to my room, shut the door,
take a seat at my desk, pull out my journal.
Six months' worth of poetry.

Sipping, I flip through the pages.
Sometimes my eyes water. Other times
laughter makes me almost spit chocolate
all over those precious poems.
So much has happened. So much.

And I can see the shape of it now—
the brief but sweet joys of summer
pivoting into the bitter struggles of fall.
The ghost of a special story
like a diamond in the rough,
an angel trapped in marble.

But what am I? I'm a poet,
my pen is a chisel of form,
able to shape thoughts and events
with meter and rhyme

till they fit together,
seamless and whole.

I down the rest of the chocolate
in a single gulp. Then, hands trembling,
I start chipping away.

PART I: SUMMER

LOS DETALLITOS

"I'll be your girlfriend."
That's what she said,
so I haven't needed
to define the relationship.

We make our feelings clear
with detallitos,
all the little things that
speak louder than words.

Like when I meet her
outside of class one day
and bend down to tie
her loose shoelace.

Or when we're walking home
and I step too close to the road
just as a semitruck speeds by,
and she yanks me onto the grass.

Or when we stop at the dollar store
and buy ingredients for spaghetti,
which we cook together at my house
because my family's at the dentist.

Or when I find her standing alone
one morning, a block from school,
looking sad, so I hug her from behind
till she leans back into me, sighing.

Or when one of Snake's minions
trips me in the hall, but she catches me,
and everyone applauds as she slowly
pulls me straight, looking into my eyes.

I'm a poet, but all these small gestures
say more than any words I could arrange.

SUNDAY MORNING AT THE TAQUERÍA

Our family is Catholic. Can't eat before
Sunday mass because of the sacrament.
So we go to the early service,
stomachs rumbling,
and try to stay focused.

By 9:00 a.m., we're hurrying
out of St. Joseph's, piling into
Dad's pickup. He almost peels out,
making Mom click her tongue
as he heads to Taquería Morales
a few blocks away.

Most Sundays, the mayor
and his wife are already eating—
they're Baptists, lucky ducks.
They can eat all they want
before church.

Mr. Morales seats us, serves
cinnamon coffee and orange juice
in cups bearing the green logo
of Club León, his favorite
fútbol team.

We order. I get my usual, chorizo
and eggs, with its sides of
fried potatoes and beans,

which I spoon into fluffy
flour tortillas along with
salsa verde.

By this time, other parishioners
come spilling in. Dad greets some,
ignores others, like his former boss.
Then in walks Joanna's father,
Adán Padilla. I try a natural smile
as he nods at my parents.

"Buenos días, Don Carlos,
Doña Judith. ¿Qué tal, Güero?"
I give a shaky wave and nod.
"¿Y su familia?" my mom asks.
"En casa. I'm picking up taquitos."

Mr. Morales hands him a paper bag
bulging with food. He pays and leaves.
Dad sips his coffee, shaking his head.
"A shame. That man should be a pillar
of the town. Güero, you looked nervous."

Mom's left eyebrow arches
the way it always does
when she gets suspicious.
"Does he not know you like his daughter?"
I shrug, my face going red. "Not sure."

I check my phone. No text from Joanna.
My parents mutter about new scandals
and old gossip. I lean forward, trying
to catch snatches, till Mom frowns.

"Cosas de adultos," she says, flicking me
back in my seat with her eyes.

"Do y'all know everyone's secrets?"
I ask, still wondering why Dad
used the word *shame*. He laughs.
"It's a small town, m'ijo. And the nosiest
folks are packed inside this taquería,
including you. Now, finish your almuerzo."

So I take another bite. But my eyes
wander across the crowded tables,
and my ears strain to hear
past clinking and laughter,
the constant heartbeat
of my community.

THE KISS

The next day,
first Monday of May,
Joanna and I take a shortcut
after school
through the orange grove
near my house.

"You know," she says,
letting go of my hand
to wipe a sweaty palm
on her black jeans,
"there's just a month
until school's out.
It'll be harder to hang out,
since my parents expect me
to help them all summer."

I stop. She turns to look at me.
There's something in her eyes
that I can feel with my chest,
which aches in a way I've never felt:
scary but good. Everything fades.

The sound of passing cars,
the harsh drone of cicadas—
all drowned out
by the beating of my heart.

The glossy green trees
and bright, dimpled fruit—

hazy, out of focus, until
all I can see are her lips,
a red I can't even describe:
dark, almost brown.

The color of mesquite pods.

Taking a shuddering breath
that feels like it might
be my very last,
I ask my fregona,
"Can I kiss you?"

She nods, slowly closing
those big brown eyes.
"Sí, Güero. You can."

So I do.

HER SONG IN MY BLOOD

My heart thunders
like a drum
when our lips meet.

Above that rhythm
I can hear
a new melody—

notes from her soul
slip into
the measures of my heart.

When we pull apart,
all I want
is to share that music,

to stand on a stage
before the world
and make them listen

to the vibrant, beautiful,
living pulse
of her song in my blood.

THEY CALL HER FREGONA

Joanna Padilla Benavides.
That's what her birth certificate says.

Padilla from her father, Adán,
who also gave her his love of cars
and lucha libre
and truth.

Benavides from her mother, Bertha,
who also gave her that wicked smile,
those beautiful brown eyes,
a big heart with quiet love,
a talent for math.

She's Jo to the twins,
six-year-old menaces
named Emily
and Emilio.

Mama Yoyo to the baby
barely learning to speak.

"I'll kick your butt if you tell anyone,"
Joanna assures me, eyebrow raised.
"My lips are sealed," I promise.
She gives me a quick kiss to make sure.

At school, of course,
they call her Fregona.

Most girls avoid her,
except for her cousins

and a few other friends
who don't quite fit in
because of gender norms
and queermisia.

Most boys are afraid of her,
at least the seventh-graders.

"I hate that nickname," she admits.
"*Güero* is positive. People think of beauty.
Even the sounds are soft and sweet.
Fregona feels rough. Ugly. Like mopping
or scrubbing grease from a dirty sartén."

"You're not ugly," I tell her.
"And there's no reason light skin
should mean beauty. That's wrong.
When I hear *fregar*, I think of the beating
you gave that loser Snake Barrera,

how you stand up for family and friends,
how you own the fresas in Pre-AP Algebra."

Joanna takes my pale hand
in her deep-brown fingers,
calloused and beautiful,
like roots in sandy soil.

"Apá keeps pushing me to be tough—
he's seen what the world does to girls."

She takes a deep breath. "He doesn't want me
to end up like his mother or sisters. Mistreated.
Ignored. And my mom's a fregona, too.
I have big shoes to fill. Can't let them down.

"But, ugh, being tough is hard. So thanks.
Seeing myself in your eyes? It helps."

She looks up, shyly at first, then smiling
like only she can smile. "And if Snake
ever bothers you again, I'll put him
in the hospital. No one touches you but me."

I put my free hand on the fist she makes,
giving her knuckles a gentle rub.

"Joanna, you don't have to be tough
when it's just you and me. I see you,
through and through, all the soft
and sweet parts, too."

Her fingers unclench as she sighs
and lays her head on my shoulder.

ROMANTIC ADVICE

After Joanna said
she'd be my girlfriend,
I was flying high like a kite.
Then the wind of reality
tangled me up with doubt.

I've never been a boyfriend.
I want to get it right,
so the next thing I did
was to ask advice
of the people I trust.

Abuela Mimi: Believe what she says
she wants from you. Take her word
about what she needs. Respect her "no"
and heed her "yes." Don't try to lead
unless she asks. Then take her hand.

Uncle Joe: Be the sort of young man
that makes her proud. Never, ever
put her down in front of others.
Never let others put her down.

Bisabuela Luisa: Music's the key.
Write her songs, sing them sweet,
never let the harmony fade
that binds your heart to hers.

Tío Mike: Love's not enough.
It's like the location and the plans.

You have to build a relationship
block by block, sweat and tears.

My big sister, Teresa: Give her space.
Don't get between her friends and her.
Don't look at other girls at all.
She deserves your loyalty and respect.

Grandpa Manuel: Give her the world.
Flowers, chocolate, necklaces—
shower that gal with gifts, Red,
till she knows she's your queen.

Tía Vero: She'll notice the little things
more than the big gestures, Güero.
Show your affection every day
in the simplest of ways.

Dad: You're like me—a fixer.
Pero, m'ijo, you won't be able to fix
every problem she has. Not your job.
Your job is to listen and comfort.
I learned that the hard way.

Mom: He sure did. At first, Güero,
each time I complained about something
that happened at work or church,
he tried to give me advice, till finally
I told him, "I can handle my issues—
I just need you in my corner, cheering
me on, lifting me up, holding me tight."

MY OWN RESEARCH

~~Before I asked Joanna to be my girlfriend,~~
~~I had spent a year reading books~~
~~and webcomics with romantic subplots,~~
~~studying the best, usually by women,~~
~~and kind of diagramming~~
~~all the ups and downs.~~

> I shaped my feelings to fit the form,
> like poetry—restrained but still warm.

> *SCRATCH THAT! REWRITE!*
> *Romantic ballad, Güero!*

Before I asked Joanna out,
I researched for a year,
read books and comics women wrote,
until that path shone clear.

Then, with my sister, I consumed
romantic shows galore—
K-dramas, telenovelas,
US rom-coms, and more!

I let the rhythms of romance
come settle in my soul.
I knew the tropes of daring love
would someday make me whole.

I won't be like those other guys,
out on a kissing quest.

Not just a decent boyfriend, no—
I have to be the best.

My girl deserves a special fate.
I want our love to *shine*.
The One True Pairing we must be
in the story of our lives.

HOW MOM AND DAD GOT TOGETHER

I tell my dad how much I fear the day
I'll finally have to tell Don Adán
I'm dating his daughter.

"I understand you perfectly,"
my dad replies. "Let me relate
the story of how your mom and I
got together and her dad's reaction.

"We had friends in common
who decided to play matchmaker
and invited us to a party. We met
and I was smitten. I just *had* to date
this beautiful woman from Mexico.
Luckily, she liked me, too.
For three months, we were inseparable,
sharing our lives and laughter,
slowly falling for each other."

This much I know, though I smile
to think of them twenty years ago,
young and passionate, weaving a love
that endures to this day.

"Your mother was in the middle
of getting her green card.

She couldn't travel home
to introduce me to her parents,
but we didn't want to wait.
So we got married here
by a justice of the peace,
nothing fancy—we agreed
to spend our money
on building a home instead.

"Once she was legally able
to return to her country of birth,
we showed up at her home
and gave them the good news.
Your Mamá Toñita was thrilled,
weeping with joy, but Tata Moncho,
well . . . he crooked a finger at me,
took me to the azotea, flat roof
under a cloudy sky.

"And, caray, he let me have it.
'Young fellow, since you've decided
to marry my daughter
without my permission,
understand: There is no return policy
in this household. You've taken her,
so take responsibility for her, too.'
Your mother overheard this speech,
was mortified, apologized.
But I got the message—some things,
Güero? You don't delay them.
Adán Padilla is a good man.
He'll accept you if you speak up.

If you wait much longer, though,
that family will feel betrayed."

My palms ache as he finishes.
My stomach flips and flops.
Yay. No pressure at all.

GÜERO Y LOS BOBBYS

Even kids who don't care crowd into
the auditorium, excited for the talent show.
Two hours free from classwork
is worth cheesy jokes, awkward dancing.

Me and the Bobbys are near the front.
We pretend we're TV judges,
mutter our advice to the contestants,
pick the performers for our made-up teams.

Joanna's cousins do a hilarious skit,
lots of slapstick humor and clever puns.
Esteban "el Chaparro" González
breaks a brick with his thick forehead.

Chesa Ossorio twirls and tosses
a glittering baton in the air,
though at the end it slips from her hand
and almost smacks the principal.

The best one is Andrés Palomares,
who loses all shyness and stammering
as he flicks his black cape mysteriously
and awes us with incredible magic tricks.

The last act is a musical group, eighth-graders
that I hardly know. They need more practice,
and the singer's out of tune. Still.
I feel a little jealous, somehow.

Bobby Delgado laughs as we leave,
a smirk on his face. "Did you hear his voice?"
And he starts to sing, imitating the boy
so perfectly, we can't help but giggle.

Then, unexpectedly, Delgado straightens
and begins to belt the song out right,
in the richest, most amazing tenor
I've heard in a long time.

Bobby Lee just stares at him, awed.
Bobby Handy rubs his eyes, shaking his head.
"Dude," I shout, grabbing Delgado's shirt.
"You never told us you could sing like that!"

Kids—mostly girls—have crowded around us.
Delgado smiles. "Pa' que veas. Hidden talents."
Then my mind goes wild with ideas. Lee plays piano
and violin. I know accordion and a little guitar.

Joanna approaches, cocking her head.
My heart beats faster as words take shape
to match the melody of our kiss. "Güero?
I know that look. What wild idea do you have?"

Reaching out to take her hand,
I turn to my friends, face flushed.
"Guys," I say, breathless,
"we've got to start a band."

WE NEED A DRUMMER

Our first try at my house is really a bummer.
It's a test for the practice we may do all summer.
Yet though we're a singer, a player, a strummer,
there's no doubt that four is the preferable number.
Staring at Handy, I sigh, feeling glummer.
My friend isn't musical. He's barely a hummer.
"Our sound is good, but it's missing another.
The beat is everything. We need a drummer."

FIRST DATE

Our first date's the work of our friends.
When we all meet to see a film,
los Bobbys and las Morras laugh—
they've bought different tickets!

Holding hands, with flustered stutters,
Joanna and I head for our seats in the dark.
The previews start. We glance around—
an empty theater.

With my fregona warm beside me,
the boring subplots fade away,
replaced by her fingers and hair,
her head on my shoulder.

When a night scene darkens the screen,
my lips find hers. The magic breaks
when a young usher clears his throat
and we yank apart fast.

"I'm hungry," Joanna whispers.
"Vamos a comer algo ya."
So we abandon the dull film
and walk across the street.

The Asian market has groceries,
but also great Korean food.
We order kimbap and japchae,
spicy tteokbokki, too.

"Our friends can be irritating,"
I say between bites. "But this time?
Got to give them props. So much fun,
just me and my girlfriend."

Joanna smiles and checks her phone.
"Ay güey. Apá will be here soon.
Let me text the girls to hurry."
A flurry of fingers.

I sigh.
It's time
to face
the music.

MEETING HER PARENTS

In the middle of May,
two weeks before school ends,
Joanna asks her parents
if I can come over for dinner.

I don't think I've been more nervous
in my entire life. Dad laughs
as he drops me off. "You're a good kid.
They know it. Just relax, Güero."

Still, sitting in the living room
facing Mr. Padilla's serious stare
is pretty intimidating.

Joanna does all the talking until
her mom calls her into the kitchen
and I'm left alone with her father,
who has many questions for me.

"¿A qué equipo de fútbol le vas?"
I explain that I'm not a big sports fan.
"Bueno, ¿qué quieres ser de grande?"
Like I'm a kid. Not sure. Maybe a writer.

"¿No vas a trabajar con tu papá
en la construcción? ¡Pero si gana bien!"
I think Arturo will inherit the business—
my brother loves to build stuff with Legos.

Mr. Padilla doesn't seem to get me.
I'm not sure he even likes me.
Throughout dinner, he keeps staring
across the table, sizing me up.

Joanna's mom asks easier questions:
my favorite foods, how school is going,
whether I've got clothes that need mending
(she's a seamstress and will fix them for free).

Then Emily taps my shoulder, head tilted.
"Are you treating Jo good, Güero?
Better not hurt my big sister's feelings."
Mr. Padilla nods. "Important question."

"Of course he is," Joanna begins,
but her mother shakes her head
as her father leans forward,
eyes peering into mine.

"Por supuesto," I finally answer,
hands shaking under the table.
"I have a lot of respect for Joanna,
and I like her too much to hurt her."

He eases back into his chair and grins.
"You pass. We maybe don't have lots
in common, but I respect her, too.
Plus, she can kick your butt, no?"

At that, the tension melts
as everyone laughs

while Joanna makes a fake fist
and playfully taps me on the chin.

Her eyes meet mine,
ever so brief,
and I nod at the real her
that glitters inside.

JOANNA AND LAS MORRAS

Just like I have my boys,
the Bobbys,
Joanna's got a clique
as well.

Kids call them las Morras.

The name started as a mean joke,
since they're not like most girls
at our school—
but they owned it.

Members:
Joanna's cousins
Dalilah Benavides and
Samantha Montemayor;

Joanna's BFF,
Victoria Castillo;

And the new inductee,
Lupe Paz, who's nonbinary
(so maybe the group should rename
itself les Morres or lxs Morrxs,
but Lupe says they don't mind)

After Joanna agreed
to be my girlfriend,

each of them approached
and threatened me.

I was expecting it.

Dalilah: "Treat her good, Güero,
or your life will get real bad."

Samantha: "Eres su primer novio.
Make her happy. She deserves it.
And you'll deserve what happens
if you ever make her cry."

Victoria: "My opinion? She's making
a mistake. You're not the right guy
for her. Pero she won't listen to me,
so try to be less of a freaking dork."

Lupe: "I can see there's something special.
So be careful with it, Güero. It's fragile,
and boys have a habit of breaking things."

I promise I will treat her well,
and I mean it, really and truly.
Joanna is everything I ever wanted
in a girlfriend. I don't plan on losing her.

ELL

Joanna's first language
was Spanish, spoken at home
and church and playground.

When she enrolled in kinder,
she was labeled "ELL"—

English Language Learner.
In her bilingual class, Spanish
was used to teach kids.

The program changed in first grade—
school board wanted English pushed.

Teachers protested:
Spanish speakers need to read
in Spanish first while

learning to listen and speak
in their second language.

But English-only
won that fight, so Joanna
fell behind in school—

forced to listen, speak, read, write, and
test in English all at once.

Her grades were not great:
She failed the reading exam,
though she's super smart.

Now, instead of English class,
she has to take ESL.

I help her study.
She's ashamed when she stumbles,
but I rub her hand.

"This is not your fault," I say.
"I'll teach you what they didn't."

JOANNA'S FIRST BULLY

In second grade,
a boy started picking
on Joanna every day.

She would wear her uniform
two days in a row so her mom
could wash and line-dry the other.

The boy called her dirty,
chompuda, and piojosa, since
her hair was usually a mess.

He laughed at her accent,
got the other kids to mock her,
stole her homework and books.

The teacher didn't notice
or maybe didn't care.
Things got worse and worse.

Then one day, in the hall,
the boy crossed a line.
He pushed her and shouted—

"I bet your mom's just like you,
stupid and dirty and prieta, too."
Tongue out, he ran into the room.

But Joanna burst into movement,
stopped the door from closing,
yanked him back into the hall.

"Di lo que quieras de mí, baboso,"
she whispered in his ear as he trembled,
"pero no vuelvas a mencionar a mi mamá."

Then she put his arm against the frame
and slammed the door. Once. Twice.
The boy howled in pain, tears in his eyes.

"I got suspended," she tells me, grinning.
"But that bully never bothered me again."

GOLFING DADS

One cool thing about meeting
Bobby Lee back in sixth grade
was our dads could reconnect.
They were high school friends,
but then Mr. Lee went to college
hours away, so they lost touch.

Now they both run businesses—
Dad's construction company,
Mr. Lee's family store.
"Pillars of the town," they joke.
Every other Saturday,
they meet up to play some golf.

Our moms aren't big fans of this
(they have lots of "honey-dos"),
and my sister, Teresa, scoffs,
"Boring and capitalist."
Bobby Lee and I don't mind—
it's so hype our dads hang out!

Once, they let us tag along,
and, whoa! A big surprise—
they spent nine holes arguing
whether Marvel or DC has
better superheroes and which
grunge band rocked hardest.

"Old fights," Dad said in the car.
"But Eugene is wrong, of course."
I couldn't keep the laughter in.
"I know two derds—diverse nerds—
who both got their geekiness
from fanboy golfing dads."

TWO MOTHER'S DAYS

A RONDEL

My mom deserves two Mother's Days,
twice the gifts, double the rest—
el mes de mayo, día diez,
and that second Sunday in May.

Mexicana in the USA,
works hard to make our home the best.
My mom deserves two Mother's Days—
twice the gifts, double the rest.

With Dad, we sweep and scrub away
and cook her favorite foods with zest.
To show we know that we are blessed,
we decorate with bright bouquets—
my mom deserves two Mother's Days.

BABY PICTURES

Despite my protests, Mom
whips out the photo albums
when Joanna's visiting.

Backward in time,
from bad hairdos
to flea market clothes.

"¡Qué chulo!" Joanna smiles.
"¿Verdad? He looks cute
in his little pink shirt!"

They're a team. Next: toddler pics!
Me, dressed like a mariachi
or showing my naked butt.

Their laughter. My blushing.
I cross my fingers that Teresa
won't barge in with comments.

"Here's his very first portrait,"
Mom says proudly.
"Un gordito enojón."

I was a big, angry baby,
face all red, fists clenched,
eyebrows knitted.

"Almost thirteen pounds!"
Mom exclaims, laughing.
"Like a Thanksgiving turkey."

Joanna pokes my ribs and laughs.
"Where did it all go, flaco?
Your brain burn all the calories?"

Mom goes to put the albums
away, leaving us to chat
at the kitchen table.

"And your hospital photo?"
I ask. "I didn't see it
in the pics at your house."

Joanna makes a smirk
that still reveals
her pretty dimples.

"My mom's a citizen,
but Apá has no papers,
which complicates things.

"Amá was working
when her water broke—
got rushed to the hospital.

"They called Apá,
and he sped over
but got stopped.

"No regular cop—
that corrupt police chief,
who threatened a report

"to immigration
unless Apá se mochaba,
paid him a stiff bribe.

"Now he drives real slow,
his eyes glued upon the road,
every mile a risk.

"Back then it was worse.
He was so nervous,
he refused everything.

"Nomás lo que es,
nothing extra,
nada que llame la atención."

It upsets her a little,
I can tell, so I hold her hand
and mutter—

"Well, I'm sure you were
a beautiful baby,
Joanna."

"Amá says I was
a scrawny, furry monster.
But thanks, bae!"

TEN THINGS I KNOW ABOUT EACH OF THE BOBBYS

Bobby Lee

1. His grandparents started their store
   when my dad was in elementary.
   They came from South Korea. Mr. Lee,
   Bobby's dad, was just a kid back then.

2. Like my own mom,
   Mrs. Lee came to the US as a teen.
   And when they speak,
   you can hear their homelands
   peeking through the syllables.

3. Bobby Lee started taking piano lessons
   when he was just three years old.
   I started the accordion when I was seven.

4. Lee and Delgado went to South Elementary.
   The Lees live in that zone. Delgado's mom
   is a teacher there, so she had him transferred.
   The two have been friends for eight years.
   That bothers me sometimes. Silly, I know.

5. His mother wants him to be a doctor,
   his father wants him to help expand
   the family business when he's older,
   but Bobby Lee isn't sure about the choices.

"I barely know what I want to do tomorrow!
Forget about ten years from now."

6. He loves his little sister, Jina, more than anything.

7. I got Bobby Lee interested in old ballads
   from Mexico's Golden Age of Music,
   and now he's obsessed with Agustín Lara.

8. He speaks Spanish better than Handy.

9. His family name
   wasn't originally Lee.
   That's just the way
   it's transcribed into English.
   In Korean, it's just "ee." Short,
   like Spanish "y." In Hangul,
   the Korean alphabet,
   it looks like a zero and a one:
   0|

10. Lee is gay. But he's only told las Morras and us—
    after our second trip to the movies this spring.
    Samantha had a crush on him, but he didn't want to hurt her
    or my relationship with Joanna. So he took a risk.
    Came out. We love him. We'll keep him safe.

Bobby Delgado
1. His mother has raised him on her own,
   since his father left one day
   and never returned.

2. Delgado wears his hair very short.
   He says, "Me da flojera to take care of it."

3. He's the funniest of us.

4. Delgado is agnostic, doesn't quite believe,
   though he has great respect for the Santería
   his mother practices.

5. Delgado is an only child,
   and he finds our family dynamics
   fascinating but foolish.

6. His parents moved to Texas
   from the Dominican Republic
   before he was born. He has
   dozens of cousins he hasn't met.

7. Delgado is proud to a fault.

8. He is an incredible artist.
   All the paintings in his home
   are his, hung by his mother.

9. He loves to read in Spanish.

10. Lee is more handsome than him,
    but the smartest girls at school
    have a crush on Delgado—
    there's something
    nerdily magnetic
    about him.

Bobby Handy

1. He adores his mother. A lot.
   Some kids call him a mama's boy.
   But Mrs. Handy is smart and cool.
   Who wouldn't want to be her friend?

2. Handy's dad is an army officer.
   He's often gone for months at a time.
   When he returns, though, he brings
   his only son tons of great gifts.

3. Handy would rather just spend time with his dad.

4. Handy has four older sisters.
   Two of them are married.
   The others are in high school.

5. The Handys are part of a big clan
   spread throughout the county.
   They all go to the same church
   one town over. They're Mormons.

6. The Handy clan is Mexican American.
   Their last name comes from a white man
   who stayed in this area after the Civil War
   and married the daughter of a rancher,
   becoming part of our community.

7. Handy and I have gone to school together
   since kindergarten. I understand him better
   than I do most of my cousins.

8. He doesn't think I know,
   but he's got a crush

on Joanna's cousin
Dalilah.

9. Handy wants to be a psychologist.
   He likes to help his friends
   with their problems.
   He gives pretty good advice.

10. Handy can't keep a beat.

AWARDS CEREMONY

Our teachers herd us to the gym,
where chairs are lined up straight and prim
while families and friends stand and wave
in the bleachers like it's a game.

The band comes marching, playing loud—
the fight song, so we all feel proud.
Then cheerleaders do a dance
to hip-hop beats while students chant.

A school board member gives a speech,
thanks parents, who have helped us reach
our every academic goal.
At last it's time to take that stroll.

One sighing homeroom at a time,
we stand and make a single line.
The principal calls us forward,
announcing each person's award.

All kids at least get a ribbon
(on the back their names are written)
for "Great Academic Efforts"
(though if that's all you get, it hurts).

When Joanna's called, I watch her
get a medal for UIL soccer,
a certificate for PE,
and cheers from all her family.

Then the principal lifts a trophy—
glittering gold—for all to see.
"Perfect score on the state math test!"
Someone mutters, "I'm not impressed."

Behind me sit middle-class girls
from Pre-AP Algebra, all snarls,
like her success has them defeated.
"The naca probably cheated."

Delgado whispers, "Dude, be chill.
Joanna's got some real mad skills.
When she's a famous engineer,
we'll see who has the right to sneer."

Handy is the star of his group:
straight As that earn him a *whoop*!,
perfect attendance, and what's more—
state medals for his test scores.

Bobby Lee, too, plus certificates
for math and science, making state.
Delgado is a reading millionaire,
best work in art, in choir first chair.

Though my attendance underwhelms,
I do get nearly everything else.
My family cheers me from the stands
as I cross the stage with a dance.

As I head back, I picture it:
In cap and gown, college graduate,
I'll lift my bachelor's diploma high
while my parents with happiness cry.

In my mind's eye, Joanna waits
for photos with me on that day:
Her mortarboard will sit askew,
her dimples always beautiful.

"You see the faces of the kids
with just the ribbon in their fists?"
Delgado asks. "No one applauds.
They look so sad. This thing is flawed."

I'm pulled back to the present time,
to note the fanfare, music, and hype.
Adults treat school like war or sports:
winners and losers, huddled in forts.

Thing is? I don't want to compete
for knowledge, where to sleep, what to eat.
There's got to be a better way—
learning and living shouldn't bring pain.

THE TORNADO AND MY BEDROOM

My parents are at my brother's school
the next time Joanna comes over.
"Bedroom door *open*," Teresa yells.

"Sorry," I say, grimacing.
"She's like my other mother.
The way you are with the twins."

Joanna nods as her eyes scan
the floor and walls of my room.
"You're a neat freak, huh?"

Then she ambles over
to the posters above my desk.
Selena and Veronique Medrano.

"Oh," she says as if discovering
some deep, dark secret of mine.
"So these are your celebrity crushes."

"More like . . . idols? Love their
voices, music, dancing . . ."
"Faces? Bodies?" Joanna adds.

I need to recover, fast.
"All I have eyes for," I say,
getting closer, "is you."

Teresa's voice booms from
down the hall. "I can literally
hear every word y'all say!"

Rolling my eyes, I sit on my bed.
"And here I thought this room
was the safest spot in town."

Joanna crouches in front of me.
"Really? What do you mean?
What did it save you from?"

"Remember the hurricane from
six years ago? The tornado passed
by this window. No damage."

Joanna's smile dissolves
as she stands and turns
her back to me.

"Oh, I remember," she says
after a long pause. Her voice
swirls with ragged emotion.

"But it didn't just pass *us* by.
It passed right *over* us,
almost destroying everything.

"Back then, my family
lived in a flimsy tejabán.
We barely survived.

"Apá tied thick ropes
to all four inside corners
to hold down our home.

"Pero Amá estaba encinta.
The twins bulged inside her.
So it was mainly me and Apá.

"We fought the twister
for a good fifteen minutes
as it tried to take our house.

"I felt myself get lifted up
like Dorothy, pero there was
no Oz waiting for me, Güero.

"So I stuck my feet
in cinder blocks and screamed
prayers to San José.

"Then it was suddenly over.
Beating the odds, we won.
Mom went into labor that night."

My chest aches for her.
But what can my privilege do
six years later? What can I say?

I just get up and hug her.
Teresa pokes her nose in
but gives us our moment.

WHAT THE HALLYU?

At my middle school,
South Korean culture
is super popular now,
especially with girls.

Dozens of K-pop fans
part of the "ARMY,"
celebrating their bias
(their favorite singer).

They stream K-dramas
and read webtoons
and shop at the Asian
market one town over.

Some are obsessed with
my friend Bobby Lee,
calling him "oppa"
(he rolls his eyes).

A few claim they know
more than he does
about South Korean
culture and cuisine.

"Maybe they do,"
he says with a shrug.
"I'm Korean American.
It's kind of different."

He struggles with Korean
but thinks that's just fine.
And his family's traditions
may not perfectly align.

Obsession isn't respect,
I have come to realize.
Some are drawn to things
they just want to possess.

Horrified, I wonder if
I'm one of those guys—
I apologize in case
I've ever crossed a line.

"You know how you always
ask me about Korean stuff?
That shows—it's, like, respect.
You don't act like you know it all."

He takes out his phone, pulls up
a playlist—Mexican techno.
Then we eat tacos de bistec
smothered in gochujang.

HANMEGSIKO SLANG!

Delgado and Handy roll their eyes
when Lee and I get started
with our favorite in-jokes—
blends of Mexican Spanish
and Korean words.

Our favorite is *kórale*,
a mash-up of Korean *kol*
(okay, cool) with its
Mexican slang synonym
órale.

We also like to say
aishiwawa,
from Korean *aish* (darn it)
and the Mexican phrase
ay chihuahua.

Bobby Lee's favorite is
heolmanches,
a blend of Korean *heol*
(whoa, what the heck)
and Mexican *no manches*.

When we're hanging out
as families, I like to tease
Arturo and Jina,
who are both in second grade
at the same elementary.

When I do, I shout, "Lero merong!"
It's a mix of the Korean taunt *merong*
and the Spanish taunt *lero lero*.
I stick my tongue out for maximum
"nanny-nanny-boo-boo"-ness.

Our English teacher, Ms. Wong,
thinks the blends are delightful!
She calls them "Hanmegsiko Sogeo"—
Korean-Mexican slang. Perfect name.
A symbol of our friendship.

WEATHER WITH JOANNA

TANKA

Wavy asphalt lines,
and the sun bleaches colors
as I start to fall.
Then my head's on her shoulders—
a sunstroke piggyback ride.

Walking one morning,
late-May rain clouds pile up dark.
Ah! My windbreaker!
A block from school, the downpour—
I cover her head, and we run!

"Can't wait for winter,"
she says unexpectedly.
"But you hate the cold!"
"Yeah, but I want to cuddle—
we can keep each other warm."

THE LAST DAY OF SEVENTH GRADE

A TRIOLET

Vacation is about to start.
It's the last day of seventh grade!
Signing yearbooks before we part—
vacation is about to start!
Some students cry from broken hearts,
while others laugh, relief displayed.
Vacation is about to start—
it's the last day of seventh grade!

THE JOURNAL

Ms. Wong hands me a journal,
leather bound, my name inscribed.
"You are a poet, my child,"
she says, eyes bright and maternal.

"No matter what happens in life,
as often as you can—just write."

SNAKE'S PROMISE

"Casas," hisses a voice
as I close my locker
for the last time.
Only one person
calls me by my surname.

Narciso "Snake" Barrera.

I turn to face the bully
who has avoided me
since Joanna crushed him.

"What do you want, Barrera?
I'm not signing your yearbook."

He nods admiringly. "Good one.
For a little white nerd. Summer.
I don't want you to enjoy yours.
So here's my promise, Casas.
We're gonna get our revenge."

I sigh, scratching my head.
"Revenge for *what*, Narciso?
Being humiliated? Really?"

"If that was all your family did,
I'd walk away from you, carnal.
But my dad helped your dad
blow the whistle on Jones Construction

back in the day. He showed loyalty.
Then your dad fired him."

"Because he was a thief!" I shout.
"Stealing from Casas Homes.
To pay off his gambling debts.
Not disloyalty, Narciso. Justice."

Snake Barrera spits at my feet.
"Say whatever you want.
But let this worry coil
at the back of your mind—
at any moment, this snake
is going to strike
where it hurts."

MY TOWN IN JUNE

A HAN-KASEN RENGA

My neighborhood teems,
alive with rambunctious shouts—
summer has begun.

La vecina, phone in hand,
glares out her window at me.

I just shrug, hefting
a cooler full of soft drinks
into our Bronco.

Somehow my little brother
is sleeping through this chaos.

The raspa man comes,
pushing his broken-down cart—
kids flock for snow cones.

Comadres in housecoats chat
beside the sidewalk, brooms poised.

And there's la Rubia,
walking to the store with an
entourage of boys.

Don Mario stands watching as
el Maistro stuccoes his house.

Doña Petra kneels
amid her blue mistflowers,
crowned with butterflies.

In the placita, old men
play dominoes, reminisce.

The next street is blocked
to serve the loud World Cup dreams
of young soccer stars.

Smiling priests—one Mexican,
one Chinese—visit widows.

Scolding, Mom hurries
my slow siblings and me
through a quick breakfast.

Amid shady mesquites,
Sara reads fate in folks' palms.

Mr. Cruz, "el Sir,"
gets to sleep in late today—
no classes, no kids.

Two dueling lawn mowers
get the city park ready.

My family piles thick
into our trusty Bronco—
the ocean beckons.

And the splendor of the sun
will light our way there.

BEACH BARBECUE

When we get to the beach,
Tío Mike is already there
with Tía Vero and my primos
Timoteo, Silvia, and Magy.
They've reserved a great spot
in the shade of the pavilion
with the biggest barbecue pit
and a perfect view of the sea.

Me and Tim help our dads unload,
while Teresa takes Arturo
and the other cousins to the water
and our moms put tablecloths down
to start preparing the food.

At first, the smoke
from smoldering mesquite
keeps the seagulls at bay,
but they're patient
and persistent.
I can see them
waiting at
the edges.

Once the meat's on the grill,
Tim wants to go play in the waves.
I'm too pale to risk it
without slathering on sunscreen—
SPF 50, like a shield against the rays.

Teresa and Silvia
have half-buried
Arturo and Magy
in the sand. I laugh.

Then Tim and I stomp into the sea,
defying the swells, jumping
to avoid the stinging salt spray,
determined to make it to the sandbar
ten yards from shore.

But the waves are too high,
come too fast, too close together,
closing ranks against us invaders.
So we finally retreat.

The little ones are unburied,
and a shaky castle is rising
from their fresh graves.
We plop right down
beside the others and help
stabilize it, widening the base.
Soon it rises taller, glorious,
encrusted with shells,
ringed by a moat.

"Enough sun for me,"
I announce, hurrying
over hot sand to rinse myself
off under the showerhead
at the bottom
of the pitted wooden ramp
that leads to the picnic area.

I towel dry just in time
to help with the final steps,
then Tía Vero goes down
to herd the kids to the tables
so we can finally eat.

Fajitas, loaded short ribs,
sausages, and chicken wings
(plus a roasted cauliflower
and nopal paddles for Teresa,
who swears she's vegetarian)
are piled high
in an aluminum pan.

"Que cada quien se sirva,"
my mom says, and we grab
paper plates, scooping up beans
and potato salad and guacamole
to accompany our favorite meats
and vegetables. Bread and tortillas
optional . . .

. . . for everyone
except the gulls, who creep closer
and closer, ready to demand
their fair share in exchange
for our presence in their territory.

GRACKLES ON THE LAWN

RUBAIYAT QUATRAINS

Rain has fallen, the sun has shone,
and all week long the grass has grown.
It's Sunday now, and our green lawn
lies there, waiting to be mown.

Dad wakes me at the crack of dawn—
we eat tacos, then with a yawn,
I yank the cord on the machine
and push it round till morning's gone.

Dozens of grackles, fluttering,
descend upon the fresh-cut green.
The name for such a flock is *plague*—
all crowded thick, they eat the seeds.

They dig for bugs, their beaks like spades,
as I rest and watch from the shade.
Then they lift like a dirty mist—
through vast blue skies, they fly away.

But strange, harsh cries come from their midst,
like echoes of the lawn mower's drone—
and I hear thanks within that groan,
as if I've helped them to exist.

TERESA'S ANNOUNCEMENT

After church one day,
when we're eating lunch
at Grandpa Manuel's
and planning the Fourth
of July party,
Teresa declares,
"I will not attend
celebrations of
any national
holidays until
Latinx people
enjoy our full rights,
representation,
and real equity
in this country called,
not America,
just the US,
since America
is the continent."

And, needless to say,
adults aren't happy
at her "radical,
woke, rebellious phase."

I hope fireworks
are still possible,
and I do not mean

the epic showdown
that's about to start
between Teresa
and Grandpa Manuel.

I'm surprised to find
he respects her choice.
"The land of the free,"
he solemnly says.
"I won't force you, girl.
But just one quibble—
what's with the *x*?"

WHAT'S WITH THE *X*?

A CONVERSATION ACROSS GENERATIONS

Grandpa Manuel:
I ain't Latinx.
I'm Tejano, Chicano,
or Mexicano.

Teresa:
Of course. I know that.
But you say *Hispanics*, no?
And *Latinos*, too.

Grandpa Manuel:
Pos, that's what we are,
put together with Cubans
and other gente.

Teresa:
Do you remember
that *men* used to mean *humans*,
including women?

Grandpa Manuel:
Yeah. That was plain wrong.
"All men are created." Dang.
I'm glad it has changed.

Teresa:
Why should *Latinos*

mean both men and women?
It's the same problem.

Grandpa Manuel:
Spanish works that way,
but I guess that's no excuse.
So did English, once.

Teresa:
Right. That's why people
are trying to change the word
by changing the vowel.

Grandpa Manuel:
But what's with the *x*?
That ain't no vowel. Hard to say.
And looks mighty strange.

Teresa:
LGBTQ
Latinx folks chose the *x*
as nonbinary.

Grandpa Manuel:
That's them as don't fit
into boy or girl boxes?
Guess they have a point.

Teresa:
They totally do.
And by tweaking the language,
we fix both problems.

Grandpa Manuel:
Fine for the US,
but what about Mexico
and other countries?

Teresa:
They're using an *e*,
so the word is *Latines*
most of those places.

Grandpa Manuel:
Ooh, I like that more.
Do you mind if I use it?
I'll follow your lead.

Teresa:
Go for it, Grandpa!
And thanks for talking this out.
Means a lot to me.

JUNTOS CON CONJUNTO

One of Dad's employees gives us
a huge crate of mangos,
too many for us to eat,
so Mom suggests we take some
to the Padillas.

I haven't seen Joanna
in nearly a week, so I agree
excitedly. We drive up the road,
turn in to her neighborhood,
with its cinder block homes
in different stages of completion.

The Padillas' place is small
but brightly painted, snug.
A half-dozen cars are parked
under or beside a big carport,
where Joanna's dad
works his mechanical magic.

We get out of the car,
head for the door, but I catch
snatches of a familiar old song—
"Mom, you go ahead.
I'll be there in a minute."
Seeing me looking toward the cars,
she nods. "Tell Don Adán hi for me."

I follow the melody, over caliche
spread upon the ground

like a royal white road
in some Maya legend.
The accordion, bass, and guitar
(no drums, the original way)
lead me to an old pickup.
Mr. Padilla's lowering the hood.

"That's 'Dime Ingrata,' no?"
I ask. "By Los Alegres de Terán?"
He squints at me. "¿Cómo lo sabes?
That's from my *father's* times,
Güero. Esta camioneta tiene
un eight-track, and that's the tape
the owner left inside."

"Oh, my bisabuela Luisa
has *all* their early vinyl records.
She's more of a balada and ranchera fan,
but she loves this kind of conjunto—
old-school norteño and Tejano music.
I've spent years listening to it with her.
Estos señores, Los Gorriones del Topo Chico,
Ramón Ayala, and even Los Donneños!"

Mr. Padilla stares at me, eyes glinting
with something new. Maybe respect?
"No sabía que te gustaba la buena música.
What about norteño from the eighties and nineties?"

Half an hour later, Joanna finds us,
huddled around a workbench,
riffling through Don Adán's cassettes,
looking for our favorite songs.

"¿Y esto?" she asks. "Since when
are you two such good friends?"

Mr. Padilla gives a raspy laugh.
"Es el poder del conjunto, m'ija.
It brings folks together."

THE VIOLIN AND THE ACCORDION

A SIJO

Lee and I know our musical styles
      must click, or there's no band.
As I lift my accordion,
      he peers at me over his bow.
Without counting, we start to play—
      perfect harmony, flawless tempo.

FINDING HANDY'S RHYTHM

Bobby Handy has no rhythm,
cannot clap to save his life.
Watch him dance, it's quite a sight—
out of sync and way too slow.

We need a drummer, though,
so I'm the lucky devil
who gets to teach this awkward boy
just how to feel the beat.

I start with basic music,
like fifties rock and roll,
it has a solid downbeat
that anyone should feel.

Not Handy, no.
His claps
keep slipping
in between the notes.

So I try to inspire him to hear
other rhythms in household appliances.
As he sits on the top of the dryer, or
leans his ear against the dishwasher.

Of course *that* doesn't work, so we
switch to the outside and listen to nature.

Droning cicadas and hastening river,
flapping of wings and dripping of dew.

In despair, I remember the primary pumping
that each of us hear when we first come alive.
Then I head to the Handys', prepared for rejection
but determined to try every last possibility.

"Mrs. Handy," I begin, "you love your son.
He loves you. But he's forgotten something.
How your heartbeat sounds. Its push and pull.
Help him hear it, ma'am. He needs that rhythm."

For one week straight, they spend each evening
watching TV on the couch. She asks him
to hold her hand, lay his head on her chest,
tapping out the pulse that brought him to this world.

Then one day he comes to practice,
sits down at the drums, and lifts the sticks—
a miracle, he starts to strike a tom
in perfect time, a thud like blood
that thunders in our veins.

LUCHA WITH THE PADILLAS

Every Sunday without fail,
the Padillas' holy grail—
lucha libre on TV,
snacks picosos flowing free!

Though it's not my cup of tea,
I have to join the fun one week.
El Dandy Junior faces off
against la Momia Karloff!

Father and daughter cheer him on,
booing and hissing at each wrong
move, every trampa and foul—
their técnico's pain makes them howl!

Then Dandy gets the upper hand,
avoids the bandages and sand,
flies through the air with awesome skill,
wrestles the rudo until he lies still.

Even I have to stand and applaud—
el Dandy Junior's a lucha god!
But my fregona's so excited,
she locks my head in a wrestling vise!

Once I've caught my breath again,
they invite me back for next weekend—

Joanna is helping her father all summer,
working on cars, crunching his numbers.
So if I want to see my bae,
I'll have to risk my neck each Sunday!

MIXTAPE FOR DON ADÁN

After several long afternoons
with Bisabuela Luisa,
learning to use old-school tech
and choosing the perfect songs,
I walk down to the Padillas'.

Though it's Father's Day,
Don Adán is hunched over
the motor of some truck,
studying its innards
like a master surgeon.

"Feliz día," I say in greeting.
"Le traje algo. Hope you like it."
I place the cassette in his hands,
weathered and smeared with grease,
hands like the men of my family,
good, honest, dependable hands.

"A mixtape? From Luisa's collection?"
I smile. "Yup. Plus a few new tracks,
favorites from Veronique, La Fiebre,
and other great acts. A ver si le atiné."

Wiping his palms clean, Don Adán
takes out the tape and slides it
into his boombox. Sweet melodies
and waltzing rhythms emerge.

"You're a good kid," he says
after a moment of listening.
"I'm glad Joanna picked you.
She has her momma's brains."

He sits down on a stool. "Got time?
I'll tell you the story of Bertha and me.
When I was barely seventeen,
I crossed the border with my primo
to get a job as a mechanic close by.
The owner gave me room and
board, me trataba bien but then
had to move away. The problem
was that I had fallen for this girl.
Bertha Benavides. Out of my league,
decían. Too smart, too pretty."
I clear my throat. "But she liked you,
didn't she? She told me you were kind,
polite, respectful. And hardworking."

"Pues sí. And that makes up for lo feo,
trust me. Women deserve to be treated
decent, like our equals, our friends.
So she picked me, Güero, and I stayed,
got a plot of land, built a tejabán,
and began fixing automobiles
under the shade of that mesquite.
We married, started a life."

I hesitate, not sure if it's appropriate,
then add, "And had a beautiful daughter."

"Así es. Though I almost didn't get
to see her born. That policía chueco
Fernando Jones pulled me over,
threatened me. Me bajó una feria
and sent me on my way."

Nodding, I try to reassure him.
"Yeah, but my dad blew the whistle.
Mr. Jones went to jail for years."

"Sure. Because what comes around
goes around. He's out now, but ruined.
That's why it's better to live a quiet,
decent life. Never step on others' backs.
And that's what I want for Joanna,
¿me explico? Keep it in mind, boy.
She picked you. Be worthy, yeah?"

HOW DELGADO GOT HIS VOICE

LINKED SESTAINS

Mrs. Delgado prayed as she gave birth
that her son be a channel for aché,
the divine force that binds heaven and earth.
The newborn opened his mouth as if to wail,
but the sounds that came out, though strong and clear,
were gentle music to everyone's ear.

My oricha's gift, she thought on that day,
ready to teach him to sing and revere.
Little Roberto soon put on display
a beautiful voice that brought the saints near.
Then his father left him without a word,
so Delgado chose not to be heard.

OUR TREE

Along the canal,
parallel to the highway,
a mesquite bosque
casts its shade over waters
that were forbidden to me.

Joanna and I
find a tall Monterrey oak,
looming majestic.
"Our tree," I say after we kiss.
The wind sighs but doesn't weep.

LA LLORONA IN
THE CANAL

Years back, when visiting Grandmother's house,
the older boys always
wanted to swim in the shady canal,
beat the heat of the day.

We younger brats were bound to tag along,
although we couldn't swim,
so Mimi tried to warn us off these plans
with a tale dark and grim.

"A pretty young woman once lived nearby,
married to a rich man
whose family rejected him because
she came from a poor clan.

"The man worked hard to support his wife and kids
(they had three in a row),
but the woman's beauty faded with time,
and working hard got old.

"So the man abandoned his wife and kids
(his mother welcomed him)
and found himself a rich and lovely bride—
a priest absolved his sin.

"The woman he had left went mad with rage
and took her children down

to our canal, wading into the murk,
letting her toddlers drown.

"Then she killed herself as well. Even hell
closed its dark gates to her,
so now she wanders that canal, searching
for her three little dears.

"If she comes across you near the water,
she'll see you as her own,
wrap you in her cold embrace, and then drop
deep and dark like a stone."

Mimi's strategy worked: We stayed away
from that weedy, ominous ditch
all summer long. Even the bigger kids
refused to scratch that itch.

The troubling tale haunted me for years.
I didn't want to learn
to swim at all, till my father made me.

Yet for years I spurned
the waters of canals.
I fear what awaits beneath
the bubble and churn.

MAKING KIMBAP WITH MRS. LEE

One day after practice,
I walk with Bobby Lee
to his house for lunch.

His mom has set colorful
vegetables out on the counter,
chopped and ready.

There's some sweet-smelling
bulgogi beef in a little bowl, too,
along with a pot of seasoned rice.

"Want to help me make kimbap?"
she asks. Bobby Lee shrugs,
but I nod like a bobblehead.

She gives us both bamboo mats
and sheets of seaweed. I watch
closely as she demonstrates.

Thin layer of rice, veggies and
beef at the bottom, lift mat
to cover, then roll, roll again.

Her practiced hands flutter
over ours, correcting form,
like my mom at the piano.

They're alike in lots of ways.
Her surname isn't Lee, like my
mom is Maldonado, not Casas.

Here Bobby's mom goes by
Hannah Lee, but she was born
Oh Ha-na, in the city of Suwon.

There's something I have
wanted to ask for a long time,
and now I muster the courage.

"What would I call you in Korean?
Sorry if it's silly or disrespectful,
but I'd be honored to try."

She smiles, pulls off a glove,
and tousles my hair. "Oh,
Güero, you're my son's friend.

"I'm his mom, his eomma,
so you can call me Eomeoni."
I know the word: *Mother*.

I feel tears prickle in my eyes.
Ducking my head, I ask,
"What's next, Eomeoni?"

FRACTURES AT PRACTICE

weird how you can
be friends for years

but put everybody
in a garage with a

wonky ac unit that
doesn't quite cool

and every disagree-
ment feels massive

none of us backs off
we want our own way

Handy's happy with
country and alt-rock

Delgado insists on
reggaeton, rap, pop

Bobby Lee has no
opinion, the dork

and I want our thing
to be electro-Tejano

so we yell at each
other and go home

VENTING TO JOANNA

me:
They don't even know why
I started it, Joanna.
Their hearts aren't in it
the way mine is—I'm driven
by the tune you stir in me.

her:
Ah you're so sweet—but
listen to them anyways
I've had my mind changed
by las morras—they're good friends
who care about you, wero

JUST WHOSE BAND IS IT?

AITA for insisting on control
of my band's musical direction?

Two months ago,
I (13M) suggested
to my talented friends
that we start a band.

Practice is held
at my house.
My dad (40M) bought
the sound system.

I took responsibility
for transforming our
clumsy friend (13M)
into a decent drummer.

He's using a small
set that's belonged to
my sister (15F)
since she was eight.

I wrote the lyrics
to our first song,
since I'm a poet,
the music, too.

The pianist-violinist
(13M) is willing to do

whatever I want, but
not the singer (14M).

Drummer is siding
with singer. Not cool.
I think they should
at least *try* my way.

But I'm worried
that this is a big
mistake, that I
might lose them.

US VERSUS THEM

A SEDŌKA

me:
You trust my taste, right?
Have I ever steered you wrong?
Please force Delgado to flip.

Lee:
This is NOT the way.
Let's sit down and discuss it
with our two rational friends.

MR. PADILLA WAKES US UP

Joanna has had enough.
She shows up at our garage,
her father in tow,
right when we're yelling
at each other.

It's kind of a dirty trick.
She knows how much
I respect him, how much
I want him to accept me.

We fall silent
as he walks in.

"A ver si entiendo,"
he begins. "Y'all
can't agree on what
kind of music to play.
Y, Güero, tú te quieres
imponer. Your ball,
your game. That right?"

I can't even bring myself
to answer, so I hang my head.

"Ain't y'all the smartest boys
in seventh grade? How come

y'all can't see the real problem?
Think about your friendship.
Y'all didn't plan that.
It just happened.
Y'all are very different
from each other,
but y'all became
something else.
A unit. Carnales."

He walks over to us, pulls us
toward him till we're standing
together.

"Let the music do the same thing.
Play what and how you like, together.
Eventually, something new,
something good, something totally
different from what's been done before
will come out of those speakers."

The solution is so simple, so perfect.
I clear my throat and look at my friends.

"Sorry, dudes. I was out of line."
Delgado puts out his hand. "Me too."
We hug it out and laugh.

Mr. Padilla is still standing there,
looking at us expectantly.

"¿Y bien? ¿Van a tocar, o qué?
Joanna's been bragging on y'all."

I pick up my accordion
and nod at Bobby Lee.
"Simple chord progression,
key of G. Basic four time,
Handy. Delgado—lyrics
are on the stand, but feel free
to improvise all you want."

Handy counts us in,
and finally
our band
starts to
play.

SUMMER SLIPS BY

A RONDELET

Summer slips by
as we practice two nights a week.
Summer slips by
as we watch shows, play games online.
I meet Joanna by our tree
near the canal when she is free—
summer slips by.

PART II: FALL

WHAT HAPPENS TO MR. PADILLA

The first day of eighth grade.
I'm waiting outside
for Joanna to arrive.

Here comes their Ford truck.
Pulls up to the curb.
Joanna gets out, smiling.

Her hair twirls, lovely,
as she turns to wave
bye to Mr. Padilla.

He drives away slow
as she runs to me,
a sweet scene from some movie.

Two black SUVs
suddenly block him,
ICE agents spilling like ants.

They're pulling him out
when she reaches me.
His voice makes her turn and scream,

"Papá!" But he's gone,
as if swallowed up
by some menacing monster.

Shaking, she fumbles
for her small cell phone.
"Oh, my God, Güero, help me."

I take it from her
shaking hands and call
her mother. I hand it back.

"¡Lo agarraron,
Mamá! Los de ICE."
Her voice breaks into harsh sobs.

By now the counselors
are herding students inside.
Then they surround Joanna.

"Let us help you, dear,"
Ms. Contreras says.
I squeeze her hands. "Go with them.

"I'll call my parents.
They know lots of people.
They'll help your mom resolve this."

Tears stream down her face
as she nods and leaves.

I stare at the empty truck,
feeling my heart break.

Then anger floods me,
and I pull out my cell phone.

SNAKE BITE

The cafeteria's a mess.
Everyone is freaking out.

Andrés Palomares rushes over,
eyes wide and red.

"Préstame tu celular," he gasps.
"Need to call my family
so they don't try and come
pick me up after school."

I give him my phone and look around.
Dozens of kids are doing the same,
scared expressions on their faces
as they think of their loved ones
or themselves.

This anger in my heart—
I'm privileged to feel it
because I'm safe from ICE.
My whole family is.

I look around at my frightened friends,
overcome by the desire to wield
my rage like a weapon or shield.
What the hell do I have privilege for
if I can't protect the ones I love?

The Bobbys find me sitting
at a table, my fists clenched,
wishing for a target.

"Güero, we just heard. Is she okay?"
I shake my head, wondering whether
she'll ever be okay again, whether
this may be the hard time that
breaks the Padillas at last.

Just then, a very tall and
broad-shouldered teen
comes sauntering over.
It's Narciso Barrera,
football quarterback,
longtime bully.

"My favorite bunch of nerds,"
he says with a cruel laugh.

"Dang, Snake," Delgado answers,
looking the jerk up and down.
"Spend all summer shooting up
steroids or something?"

"We can't all be scrawny wusses."
Snakes sizes us up. "Y'all grew a bit,
though. Almost didn't recognize
el Chino."

Lee scoffs, shaking his head.
"I'm Korean American, moron."

"Yeah, but that doesn't work for me.
Y'all's nicknames have to fit together.
Like a clique, you feel me? El Güero,
el Chino, el Pocho . . ."

Handy narrows his eyes.
"Hey, what the—"

". . . and el Ne—"

Delgado grabs Snake's shirt.
He's almost as tall
as the bully.

"I don't think you want
to finish that sentence,
Snake. I'll make you
beat me up, and you'll get
suspended from the team."

Snake lifts his hands
in mock surrender.

"Don't get your panties
in a bunch, Dominicano."

There's suddenly a disturbance
near the office. I look over to see
Joanna exiting. Her cousins
and friends meet her, start
walking toward us.

Pulling Delgado's hands
from his shirt, Snake turns.

"And here's la Fregona
with las Morras. Joanna!
How're you holding up?
Ain't payback a b—"

I jump to my feet.
"You didn't!"

Snake's mouth spreads wide
in a reptilian smile.

"Oh yes,
Casas.
I did."

He swivels back to Joanna.
"Thirteen years in the making,
morenita. Your dad got stopped.
Tried to bribe a cop. But Jones"—
Snake starts to cackle—"he wrote it up.
A ticket. Speeding. Evading arrest."

The twist of emotions
on Joanna's face
smashes my heart
to pieces of blazing ire.

"¡Hijo de la gran—!"
I shout, rushing Barrera.
He easily grabs my wrists
and keeps me at arm's length.

"Y'all are so damn smart:
Know what happens
when you don't pay a ticket?
They issue a warrant.
If you're an illegal
and keep ignoring it,
that warrant becomes
a deportation order."

Snake shoves me away.
Joanna catches me
before I go sprawling.

Then the bully lifts three fingers
counting off the words he spits.

"Game.
Set.
Match."

TRYING TO COMFORT JOANNA

I keep expecting a rumble,
but Joanna weeps and mumbles,
"I protect, he takes revenge—
now the circle never ends."
Before things get worse, I act,
take Joanna aside with tact.
I'm no fighter. It's not my place.
I need to keep my girlfriend safe.
She sinks into my firm embrace.
"We've got your back. Forget this güey,"
I whisper gently in her ear.
"Your dad's lived here for twenty years—
there's bound to be a path for him."
She pulls away, her features grim.
"I hope you're right, but look around.
Hate's taken root in our own town,
in our own people, infected minds
believing lies, looking to find
someone to blame for their problems."
She's right. This is no mere squabble.
Our whole country is fracturing.
"And your mom? How is she handling
the arrest? Did my dad call her?"
Joanna nods. "Your mom offered
to watch the kids. But I'm going home
soon. Don't want them to feel alone."

THE ASSEMBLY

As me
and las Morras
and los Bobbys
walk Joanna to class,
the intercoms chime.

"Homeroom teachers,
please escort your students
to the gymnasium for an
important assembly."

All nine of us turn around,
not waiting for teachers,
and show up first.

The counselors guide us
to the bleachers, then
everyone else files in,
buzzing with nerves,
fear, confusion.

The superintendent
and principal speak,
trying to reassure us
that the school district
will keep us safe,
that there is nothing
to worry about.

Joanna sucks air in,
trying not to cry,
shaking her head.
I take her hand—
she squeezes tight.

Then, as the counselors
give information on
who to contact with
legal questions, there's
movement at the entrance.

Mrs. Benavides gestures,
and Joanna lets go of me,
stands up without a word.
The whole gym goes quiet
while we watch her leave.

TEXTING THAT NIGHT

her:
I'm going to kill snake
he wasnt joking—his dad
and the corrupt cop
that once caught my dad speeding
worked with friends in la migra

me:
They both have broncas
with my dad, too—hurts us both,
but your family more.
Focus on saving your dad.
Snake's a lost cause, Joanna.

her:
That's easy for you to say
but dont tell me what to do

me:
I was out of line.
Please forgive me, Joanna.

her:
The baby's crying, good night

THE STAY

The next day, Joanna stays at home.
I can barely focus on my lessons.
My heart aches; my stomach feels queasy.
None of the teachers make an impression,
especially with all the beginning-of-the-year
boring routine. I just simmer in my emotions.
Right after lunch, I get a text from Joanna.

> My dad was just about to be loaded
> on a bus for mexico when mr paz—
> that's lupe's dad, he's a lawyer—
> got a judge to stop them—emergency
> stay of deportation, it's called
>
> Now they're sending him to the regional
> detention center—we'll be able to call
> him every day and visit him two times
> a week while we wait on the process

BACK ON CAMPUS

By Thursday, Joanna's back.
Her eyes are puffy and red
from all the crying she does
            alone
where no one can see her.

"We visited him yesterday,"
she tells us during lunch.
Her jaw tightens so much,
I can hear her molars grind
against each other.

"It's like a jail.
Uniforms, guards,
bars, chains. But
my dad is no criminal.
He just doesn't have papers,
like hundreds of people
in this town. Arrest them?
Why? Who are they hurting?
They can't take anything
from us or the government.
All they do is contribute!"

We agree it isn't fair.
But what can we do?
We're in middle school.
We don't make the laws.
No one will listen to us.
Will they?

POETRY UNIT

A SONNET OR WHATEVER

Our English teacher is Mrs. LaPrade,
an older woman, strict and serious.
She holds a master's, has studied abroad,
and strides through the room all imperious.

"Today begins our poetry unit,"
she announces with a devious look.
"Which of you can succinctly review what
poesy is without consulting the book?"

"It's the clearest lens for viewing the world—
a rich yet musical tool for all folks."
She twirls to stare at me, clearly unnerved.
"Ah, Mr. Casas, enough of your jokes.

"Poesy is difficult, dark, and complex.
One needs much study to truly connect."

I'M NOT MR. CASAS

HEROIC QUATRAIN

You say you want to show respect, pero
I sincerely wish you wouldn't bother.
Like everyone else, just call me Güero.
I'm not Mr. Casas; that's my father.

IT'S NOT CASTELLANO

I don't know what the deal is
with adults this year,
but our Spanish teacher,
Mr. Ramos,
is just as arrogant
and annoying
as Mrs. LaPrade.

He has us
describe
our families
in Spanish
to gauge
how good
we speak.

When it's Handy's turn,
he stumbles, then says,
"Mi llamo Roberto Handy.
Orita yo y mis four sisters
y mis papases estamos viviendo
anca la güelita
pa' que los roofers
tengan chance de hacer repair
el roof de nuestra casa."

"I don't know what you're speaking,"
Mr. Ramos tells Handy with a smirk,
"but it's not Castellano."

I raise my hand,
tired of sarcasm
and abuse.

"A ver, joven, ¿tiene una pregunta?"

"No, Profesor. Una explicación.
Lo que hablamos aquí
no es castellano.
Es español mexicano.
Y mi compañero emplea
el dialecto fronterizo
que todos los presentes
entendemos sin problemas.
Usted también, me imagino."

Face turning red,
Mr. Ramos returns to his desk
and pulls out a form.

"A referral," someone whispers.
There's a wave of *whoas*.

"No way. Güero's getting
sent to the office? Dang!"

My palms ache
as I watch him scratch
furiously across the page.

Speaking up
has a price.

IN THE PRINCIPAL'S OFFICE

HEROIC COUPLETS, SORT OF

Mr. Almaguer:
Sit down, Güero. I've been wanting to chat.
I know you're mad about Joanna's dad,
but many of your teachers are worried
about your attitude. If you should need—

me:
It's not just that, sir. It's like I can see
the "cosas de adultos" y'all keep from me.
What I've found behind the mask of this town
is breaking my heart. I can't keep it down.

Mr. Almaguer:
You're growing up. No one is perfect, son,
but it hurts when childish dreams come undone.

me:
Okay, fine. But we should at least expect
more from our teachers. A bit of respect.

Mr. Almaguer:
Apologize first, then
I'll address it with them.

WHAT'S YOUR REAL NAME?

Rebecca Mijangos,
seventh-grade leader
of our school's Chicana
K-pop fandom,
catches Bobby Lee and me
in the library one morning.

Sitting down at our table,
she leers at him and asks,
"Oppa, what's your real name?"
With a deep sigh, he replies,
"Robert Lee. That's what's printed
on my birth certificate."

Rebecca pouts. "You don't have,
like, a secret *Korean* name?
Something really cool
that only family uses?"
Before Bobby Lee can answer,
I slap the table, angry.

"Why aren't you asking *me*
what *my* real name is?
Everyone calls me Güero,
pero es solo un apodo.
Why single him out? It's gross,
can't you see that?"

Fuming, she gets up and smirks
at me. "A nadie le importa
tu estúpido nombre, Güero.
You're not cute like Oppa.
And you've got a girlfriend."
She storms off, muttering.

"How do you put up with it?"
I ask Bobby Lee. "So annoying.
Maybe they'd stop obsessing
if you came out to everyone."

The look of betrayal on his face
knocks the wind from me
like a punch. I suddenly understand
why people in dramas drop
to their knees to beg forgiveness.
"Oh, my God. I'm so sorry, Lee.
That was out of line and mean.
None of this is your fault.
I'm just . . . just . . ."

"I know, Güero. I know.
No worries, brother."
But his back is tense
when I try to hug him,
and he slowly pulls away.

PHONE CALL WITH PAPÁ

Joanna stops going to judo.
Her grades are dropping,
even Pre-AP Geometry.

One evening I show up,
insisting she let me tutor her
at the kitchen table.

"I can handle it," she insists,
listless and irritated.
"I'm not dumb, you know."

Before I can protest,
her phone rings.
It's from the jail.

Tears well in her eyes
as Joanna sets the phone down.
"Apá wants to be on speaker."

"Hey, Güero," Don Adán says.
"My wife tells me acá mis ojos
is falling behind in schoolwork."

"I'm here to tutor her, sir."
Joanna lifts an angry hand,
stopping my response.

"Talk to *me*, not *him*, Apá.
I'm not his responsibility.
He doesn't decide what I do."

There's a moment of silence.
I swallow heavy, feeling shame
spread through my gut.

"Sorry, m'ija. You're right. Still—
my life's in time-out right now,
pero you've got your future ahead.

"I know there's pressure,
sé que le ayudas a tu amá,
pero don't give up what you like.

"Pasa tiempo con tus amigas,
play games, get Güero to take you
to the movies. And study, m'ija.

"Vas a ser una mujer importante.
Engineer. Architect. Something big.
Don't let this derail you, hear me?"

Joanna nods, crying softly.
"Está bien, Apá. I promise.
Pero cuídese. We need you."

LAS MORRAS

So many kids try to reach out
and help Joanna with whatever,
but she's already got a crew
that can handle nearly anything.

Dalilah Benavides is our town's
most famous influencer—
her videos on chola makeup
keep going viral.

She's got tens of thousands
of followers who adore her
and who she can mobilize
if she wants or needs to.

Samantha Montemayor is fearless.
She rides a scooter all over town
and will enter the motocross circuit
next year to race on dirt bikes.

That love of motorcycles is a family trait—
her mom and her uncles participate
in the motorcycle rally
at the beach each year.

Victoria Castillo is an amazing cook,
whipping up all sorts of delicious food
at her parents' little restaurant
by the expressway.

She always jokes that she won
Joanna's friendship by preparing
the best pozole (my fregona's favorite)
this side of the border.

Lupe Paz is great at debate—
they can take the argument
of any cocky opponent
and tear it to shreds.

They got their insight
from their dad, the lawyer
who represents Don Adán.
His record is sterling.

LA MECÁNICA Y
EL TRAIDOR

There are five pending cars
in the Padillas' yard.
Joanna needs to fix them quick
before the owners come take them
to some other garage.

She asks for help from us,
los Bobbys y las Morras,
and we spend two weekends
as her eight assistants
so the job's less enormous.

Samantha knows engines;
Victoria and Lupe learn fast.
The rest of us do what we can—
we're surprised that Handy
is really quite handy!

But our work's just not enough.
Then a voice speaks, all gruff—
"Can I help? I've got skills."
It's Esteban González.
El Chaparro, Snake's bud.

"I live just down the street,"
he explains. We don't greet
him. Joanna spits, sighs.

"Tell me, Chaparro, why
would you ever help me?"

"Porque son fregaderas,
Fregona. Mis jefes
are undocumented, too—
can't let Snake do this to you.
We need some real vengeance."

"Be a mechanic now,"
she commands with a scowl,
"then we'll see what comes next.
If you earn my respect,
you can tell me how."

The traitor starts to work.
I pull out my journal
and reread her words:
"I protect, he takes revenge—
now the circle never ends."

A LA RU-RU

After the repairs are done
and clients have all paid,
Joanna helps her mother sew
the clothes that were delayed.

Almost every evening,
I go to watch the kids
until they slip into dreams
beneath their heavy eyelids.

One night, Baby Mari
just won't settle down,
so I take her in my arms
and rock her to this sound:

> A la ru-ru, Mari,
> a la ru-ru ya.
> Duérmete, mi Mari,
> duérmeteme ya.
>
> Esta niña linda
> se quiere dormir,
> pero ese sueño
> no quiere venir.
>
> Esta niña linda
> que nació de día
> quiere que la lleven
> a ver a su tía.

Esta niña linda
que nació de noche
quiere que la lleven
a pasear en coche.

A la ru-ru, Mari,
a la ru-ru ya.
Duérmete, mi Mari,
duérmeteme ya.

When she's fast asleep,
I lay her in her crib.
My voice is not the greatest,
but I give what I can give.

PRONOUNS

One of our teachers, Mr. Ross,
asked for our pronouns when
school began. Several others
respect us when we share them,
take good care to use the right ones.

Want to make a guess as to who
flatly refuses? Right. LaPrade
and Ramos. That means Lupe
gets misgendered every day.

As a sort of protest, I convince
all the students in both periods
to write their pronouns atop
every piece of paper submitted.

When they call roll, we all say
"Present, he/him" or whatever
our pronouns happen to be.
Maybe the teachers won't
change, but we can make
sure they never forget us.

LUCKY TO BE IN ESL

I'm sitting outside the principal's office
for the second time this year and in my life
when Joanna comes walking by.

I feel pretty foolish as she heads my way,
scowling and shaking her head. She takes a seat
beside me and demands an explanation.

"Sometimes I think you're lucky to be in ESL,"
I tell her. "Because you don't have to deal
with Mrs. LaPrade's old-school literary nonsense."

"No manches, Güero. What dumb thing
are you arguing about with her today?
Didn't I tell you just to let her say whatever?"

"She's making us read a bunch of old books
by white authors, with no modern stories for kids
like us for balance. Now students hate literature."

"I get that. But what did *you* do? Bring a comic?"
I shake my head and laugh. "Today was grammar.
She wrote a sentence on the board."

I make sweeping motions. "'The blanket of stars
spread over the countryside.' Then she asked us
what the complete subject was."

Joanna thinks for a second. "It's 'the blanket of stars,'
right?" I nod. "Yup. But then she asked us
what the *simple* subject was. Olga said 'stars.'"

Joanna narrows her eyes. I shake my index finger.
"That's wrong. But Mrs. LaPrade clapped her hands
and said Olga had it right. So I had to intervene."

"No, you didn't," Joanna says, sighing. "But you did."
"Of course I did! I'm not going to let the other kids
learn grammar wrong, bae. I corrected the teacher.

"I said, 'No, ma'am. The simple subject is *blanket*.
The noun *stars* is the object of the preposition *of*.
The prepositional phrase *of stars* describes the subject."

Joanna rolls her eyes. "Let me guess. She shushed you,
but you wouldn't shush, ¿verdad que no? Ay, Güero."
I pick up the referral form from the other seat. "Yup."

"¿Cuándo vas a aprender, flaco? People's problems
are their own. Ya sé—your family told you to use
your privilege for good. But there are limits, güey.

"Pero bueno, since you think ESL is so much better,
dile al director que te ponga conmigo in my class. Ha!
¿No que no? Didn't think so! OMG. There are bigger battles."

LIMBO

The wait is the worst,
her dark eyes sinking deeper
from all the nightmares
that rob her of peace and sleep,
leaving just anguish to share.

I have action plans,
I have recommendations,
but I bite my tongue and listen
like my parents taught me to,
eyes locked on hers, leaning close.

I open my ears,
let her grief pour into me
so she can
at least
breathe.

LET'S ORGANIZE

After a month of "legal wrangling,"
Mr. Paz, the Padillas' lawyer,
wants to galvanize public support.

He arranges interviews
with the local affiliates
of CW and Univision.

Reporters talk to Mrs. Benavides,
but it's Joanna and the twins
who light a wildfire with their words.

"You take a man who works hard,"
Joanna says, fierce eyes streaming tears,
"is loved by his community, respected,
churchgoing, honest—and you treat him
like a criminal, take him from his children
and his wife. How is that family values?"

The clip goes viral. Los Bobbys team up
with las Morras again to create and manage
social media accounts called "Free Adán."

Dalilah does a great explainer video,
teaching chola eyeliner techniques
while breaking down the injustice
and pointing her fans at our handles.

We film a debate between Lupe
and Lucas Higuera, president

of the local Young Republicans.
Lupe vivisects his anti-immigrant stance.

Soon we've got thousands of followers.
Many are asking what they can do.

We brainstorm ideas, then approach Joanna.
"Let's organize," I say. "Something big."

JOANNA'S RELUCTANCE

her:
I don't know, wero
too big, too much attention—
could backfire on us

me:
Bae, Mr. Paz said
we need the public angry
to convince judges.

her:
You're pushing too hard
my dad's the one who gets hurt
if you're wrong, you know

me:
We've got this, I swear.
Everyone is on our side.
Trust me, Joanna.

PLANNING

There's an infectious sense
of excitement as friends and family
come together with all our tools
to fight for a worthy cause.

First, our parents take the lead.
My dad gets a permit for the protest,
to be held at the city park,
across from the immigration court.

The Lee Family Store
is two blocks away,
and they provide materials
for signs, water, and snacks.

Victoria's family
will sell BBQ chicken plates
to raise money to pay
the legal fees.

The Handys know our mayor,
Alicia Montoya. They ask her
to give some brief remarks,
and she agrees.

Mrs. Delgado organizes teachers
who are brave enough
to speak out against
such injustice.

Teresa promises to bring
the high school's entire LSA,
Latinx Student Alliance,
several dozen teens.

I've been to some protests before,
but this is my first time starting one.
My feelings for Joanna and Don Adán
make a knot in my throat.

At last I get to do something for them.
Now they'll see what they mean to me.

PROTEST

On the day of the protest,
about two hundred people
fill the park, waving signs
that read FREE ADÁN.

Energy crackles through the crowd
like eager flames of fervent fire,
leaping from heart to heart—
a blaze of righteous indignation.

My tíos are there, my abuela as well—
plus tons of kids from our school.
Everyone's thinking and feeling the same.
Together, it's like we're sharing one soul.

Joanna says she's shocked
by all the support.
I can see hope growing
in her wounded heart.

Opening remarks from Mr. Paz,
then Mayor Montoya addresses
the crowd and the gathered media,
calling for Mr. Padilla's release.

Leaders of teachers' associations,
businesspeople, the superintendent,
and even a school board member
take the mic to support us.

But then, as Mrs. Benavides
thanks the protestors
and begins to give an update,
a caravan of trucks arrives.

American flags flutter beside
red banners reading
MAKE AMERICA GREAT and
BUILD THE WALL!

Doors open and
hate spills out.

BACKLASH

It's an ugly counterprotest
by folks who think that they know best.

Since our state allows open carry,
they display their guns, acting scary.

They've got signs, embossed with eagles:
AMERICA FIRST and NO ILLEGALS.

They chant "Protect our borders!"
and throw our protest out of order.

Some are white, but most "Hispanic,"
so their attack is more traumatic.

One woman loses her calm,
starts shouting at my mom.

An older gent, army vet,
waves his rifle like a threat.

A few of the armed adults
confront us kids with insults.

Lee gets cornered by three women:
"Go back to China, Ho Chi Minh!"

Delgado screams at one big dude,
"Hit me if you think I'm rude!"

Joanna grabs at a sign that reads
DEPORT PADILLA FAMILY!

Uncle Joe snatches a bat
from a camouflaged man's hands.

At last, Samantha's family arrives,
wearing black leather, throttling bikes.

Then some fool pulls out a chainsaw,
and the police lay down the law.

Everyone's at last dispersed,
but that attack was just the first.

TROLLS

By that evening, Mr. Padilla's
Wikipedia page is taken down
by editors who say he's "not notable."

Then free-adan.org is hit
by hackers who make the site
unavailable to possible donors.

Trolls flood our social media posts
with hundreds of crude comments
until we're forced to lock all accounts.
Cruel emails keep rolling in for hours.

"This feels coordinated," Handy says,
trying to use his computer skills to keep
everything running. "Someone sicced
these jerks on us like rabid dogs."

Videos of the clash are all over,
and people dox not just the adults,
but us middle-schoolers, too.

Soon Joanna and me,
los Bobbys, and las Morras
are getting smeared everywhere.

SOME TIME FOR MYSELF

When real despair comes
it's over a video call
on a shaky connection.

"I told you," Joanna said.
"But you think you know better.
You think you have the answers.
You think you can solve this.
You're a thirteen-year-old *boy*,
Güero. You can't stop a system
that has worked like this for years
or the evil men that know
how to use it for their goals."

My hand grips the mouse
like a grenade, trembling.
"What you're asking is hard,
Joanna. Maybe too hard for me."

"All I'm asking is for you
to be by my side through this.
But maybe you're right.
Maybe that is too hard.
Maybe I'm in this alone."

I can barely see the tears
streaming down her face
through the blur of my own
relentless weeping.

"Joanna, I'm sorry.
I promise I'll stop."

Wiping her face, she nods.
"Maybe you will.
Until then, I need
some time for myself.
Don't call till I call you."

Then she ends
the call,
trapping
my heart
inside.

WHAT HAPPENS TO THE LEE FAMILY STORE

A week after the protest
something so horrible happens
that it's almost impossible
to believe.

The Lee Family Store
is vandalized, windows broken,
red graffiti sprayed all over
brick walls.

Go back to China
is the least offensive of the comments.
I can't bring myself to write
the rest.

The Lees are devastated,
angry, confused—four decades
they've lived in this little border
town.

Has this hatred always been here,
waiting for the right moment
to spew from the cracks
in civility?

Nearly everyone turns out
to help clean up the glass,

scrub away the paint, apologize
to the owners.

We show our solidarity
as best we can, but something
is broken now. Bobby Lee
sums it up:

"We thought this town was safe,
that we were allies with y'all.
But now?

"Some of y'all want us to leave,
like some want Mr. Padilla deported.
It hurts. It's sad. And ironic—

"we should be standing *together* against
the folks who want *all of us* gone.

WHAT'S WRONG WITH OUR TOWN?

I go with Uncle Joe to the ranch,
trying to wrap my head around
the events of the past few weeks.

Angry, I drop onto a mesquite stump.
"When did our people get like this?
What's wrong with our town?"

"Ay, m'ijo, ain't you been
listening to my history lessons?
It's been this way for more
than a century," he explains.

"I know it *used* to be bad . . ."
I begin, but Joe shakes his head.

"Look at the land our town sits on.
First it was the motherland
of several Coahuiltecan tribes,
killed or converted by the Spanish,
whose king parceled it out as gifts
to rich families. Over time,
it became large ranches
as Mexico emerged,
growing smaller
when the border
crossed over us.

"Then white folks came
from the north and east,
bought up the land,
established this town,
pushed us mexicanos
south of the tracks.

"It took many decades,
but nuestra gente rose
to take the reins
of our community
once again."

Now it's my turn
to interrupt—

"That's what I mean!
I thought we were special,
thought we had learned
from all that oppression
to live with dignity and respect."

Joe shrugs, spreading his hands.
"Many of us did. Maybe most.
But all you have to do is check
our votes in the last election
to see how low a bunch
of us have stooped.
Some folks want whiteness
so badly, want that power,
they'll turn their backs
on their own gente."

My mind flickers with images
of Joanna, silent for days now,
and all the violence done to her
as a morena living in a colonia
who won't bend her head.

My head hurts as I realize
my trust was built on lies.

Why couldn't I see
the flaws in the jewel
I believed my town to be?
Because I'm thirteen?

Or because they're well hidden
by older folks who hope
we'll all forget
to remember?

EPIPHANY IN MY YARD

House looms, imposing—
thick emerald grass spreads like wealth
across the acres.

A few blocks away,
their home awaits, unfinished—
ruins of a dream.

SENDING JOANNA POEMS

On Valentine's Day
she revealed the answer,
but I was too stubborn
to comprehend.

"Hold my hand,
write me a poem."

That's all she ever asked.
So I will sit at this desk
with my helpless heart
and send her what she needs.

THESE HANDS

These hands are not my grandfather's hands,
gnarled and corded, cratered with sores,
crisscrossed with lines and cement burns
that chart six decades of plastering toil.

These hands are not Don Adán's,
small but powerful, eternally stained
by engine grease and gasoline,
gentle enough to hold a joyful baby.

Slender, clean, nails clipped to the quick—
my hands dance across keyboards,
computer and accordion both,
spinning out words and sounds.
One day I hope they will as well
belong to a master craftsman.

ECHOES

At practice today,
our first rehearsal in weeks,
we were all immersed
in a wall of cumbia sound
and began to improvise.

Then Delgado frowned
and started singing a song
we all know by heart.
"Mi fantasía"—a tune
Don Adán would often hum.

We stopped playing then,
our hearts thrumming with echoes
of the melodies
that bind us to an elder
who we all respect and love.

For me it was more poignant—
his daughter's laughter echoed
in each aching word.

"Tan solo de pensar
que te vuelva a besar,
mi corazón nervioso está
late que late."

THE OLD WITCH
AND THE FLOWER CHILD

A FOLKTALE FOR JOANNA AND LAS MORRAS

The old witch pinched
the flower child
and told them true:
"This flesh you wear?
It isn't all of you."

Tears came streaming
from the flower child's eyes
as they softly cried:
"That's all that others
can ever see of me."

The old witch laughed
and spread her arms.
"Ah, there you're wrong,
For in our souls
is something strong."

Bursting with plumes,
she transformed into
a horned owl, hooting:
"I'm a bird of the night!
Show me . . . what are you?"

Trembling with fear,
the child felt themself
blossom at last.

Sloughing off the old mirage,
they stood, revealed,
and began to laugh.

SITTING WITH
THE HARD TRUTH

Every time I tried to make you smile,
did I worsen your pain all the while?
It's not fair to force you toward good cheer—
there's a reason for sadness, anger, and fear.

But understand—to just be by your side,
sweetly and lovingly there to abide,
feels like I'm trying to shake myself free
from some unspoken responsibility.

Still, I'm learning to be more like you,
mouth shut, sitting with the hard truth.

I FEEL SO PROUD OF YOU

A SESTET

I feel so proud of you, Joanna dear.
You hold your head high even when the tides
of life come swirling fast. You persevere.
I promise I'll keep standing by your side,
for though you're strong enough to bear the weight,
when you're in need of rest, my arms await.

SUPPLICATION

To err is human.
To forgive, divine.
You're like a goddess
enshrined in my heart—
will you forgive me
for doubting your power?

MAKING UP

She finds me in the library,
a half dozen poems in her hand
like a bouquet plucked
from the garden of my soul.

"Yes," she whispers.
The word is a key
turning in the lock
hanging from the hasp
of the solid door
that has kept us apart.

She flings it wide open
with a kiss.

MONEY PROBLEMS

It's so expensive to fight injustice
within the legal system.
On top of everything else,
her family's running out of money.

"If it were tax season,"
Mrs. Benavides says,
"Joanna and I could help
people file for a fee."

They do what they can,
extra sewing, a car or two,
watching the neighbors' kids,
accounting for a few small businesses.

The early donations have all been used,
but the bills keep piling higher and higher,
as if that's the point—to make people give up
so that the system can roll on forever and ever.

LUISA'S IDEA

I'm at Bisabuela Luisa's house,
listening to old norteño
and Tejano records,
feeling sad,
learning to live
with this discomfort.

"¿Cómo va lo de don Adán?"
she asks, patting my hand.

Before I know it, all my pain
comes pouring out in words.

My bisabuela hugs me,
then gestures at her albums.
"It strikes me that the answer
to the money problem is clear.
Adán Padilla loves music.
Everyone does.
And, m'ijo, they'll pay
to see it played live.
So many bands
en esta comunidad."

It takes me a minute,
but then I understand.
"A benefit concert?
Tejano and norteño?"

Excitement bubbles up,
burbling bright at a chance
to smooth a problem down.

But I stop myself.
I've learned my lesson.

"It can't be me," I tell Luisa.
"I've already forced that family
into more suffering—twice."

With a wink, she reaches toward
her old-school landline phone.
"Very wise. Let me talk to Bertha.
If she approves, I'll take charge."

JOANNA'S REQUEST

After a spate of autumn rain
has swollen the canal to its edge,
Joanna texts me to meet her
under our Monterrey oak.

She's wearing a floral skirt
and sleeveless embroidered blouse.
For a moment she seems a dryad
or lovely chaneque, forest sprite.

She hugs me tight, gives me a kiss,
then, smiling, tells me her news:
"Amá is organizing a concert
to raise money for Apá's defense!"

It turns out that the Benavides clan
has connections to local conjunto.
And Joanna's aunt Xochi deejays
for a Tejano radio station.

"They're lining up great groups, Güero!
I made *just one* request. Hope it's okay."
She bites her lip, then punches my shoulder.
"You and los Bobbys get to perform!"

"Wait, what?" But she's pressed a finger
against my lips. "Guess who's headlining?
Guess who's a fan of Dalilah's videos
and has agreed to meet you in person?"

My mind is whirling. All I can do is shrug.
"Veronique Medrano, bae. Girl on your wall.
She'll be performing some of Apá's favorites,
along with her original songs. Chido, ¿no?"

Forget that Luisa came up with the idea.
My girlfriend is smiling. Happy.
Bequeathing a gift I'd never dare dream.
In control of something, bringing joy.

I'm overcome with roiling emotion,
a strange blend of excitement and guilt.

My band of thirteen-year-old boys
only gets to play with all these pros
in November at the Livestock Grounds
because my girlfriend's suffering.

That bittersweet silver lining
you always hear about,
the kind you only find
when you're standing
at the very center
of the dark cloud.

HALLOWEEN OBSTACLE COURSE

No trick-or-treat for me this year;
instead I'll bring the pingos FEAR!

Los Bobbys help me decorate—
the garage becomes a creepy place!

To reach the candies, kids must run
past screeching owl and scary nun,

avoiding spiders and hairy claws
that from the dark black ceiling drop!

Then guarding the candy stand two fiends:
La Llorona and El Cucuy!

Any huerco that makes it that far
will get two full-size candy bars!

As they're heading out, one more fright:
Dad in a hockey mask, what a sight!

Cast:
Bobby Handy as *La Lechuza*
Bobby Lee as *Scary Nun*
Bobby Delgado's Hands as *Two Manos Pachonas*
Teresa Casas as *La Llorona*

Güero Casas as *El Cucuy*
Carlos Casas as *The Masked Father with a Beer*
Judith Casas as *The Eternal Refiller of Candy Basket*
Arturo Casas as *Kid Trick-or-Treating with Cousins*

DÍA DE MUERTOS

It's been two years since Great-Grandpa died,
so Teresa insists we make an altar
to greet and honor Jorge Casas
and to remind Bisabuela of their love.

Grandpa Manuel is at first opposed.
"This Tejano family never ever
celebrated Day of the Dead before.
It's a recent import from Mexico."

But Teresa knows how to talk to him.
"You're not wrong. Our traditions were erased
by US schools and white hegemony.
Still, we can choose to recover them, right?"

As I predicted, she wins the fight.
Soon most of the family is pitching in,
finding the right photo, decorating,
discussing his favorite foods and drink.

Dad picks up Luisa for family lunch,
and she is delighted at the marigolds,
the bright papel picado, the tamales
and tequila her beloved adored.

She takes his photo in her shaking hands,
holds it tight against her chest, whispering,
"Mira nuestra familia, Jorge—
kind folks who love us dearly. We did good."

THE BENEFIT BEGINS

The stage looms.
More than a thousand people
throng together in the crisp air
of our first cold front.
Xochi addresses the crowd
in her fast Tex-Mex DJ patter,
amping them up,
making them cheer,
keeping them warm.

Then images of Adán Padilla
and his family
flash upon the screen
as an aching ballad
gives voice to our
collective grief
over the loss of something
words alone
could never name.

THE PARADOX OF THE STAGE

After a few more words,
Xochi Benavides shouts,
"Demos la bienvenida a la
middle-school sensation
Güero y los Bobbys!"

Joanna hugs me tight.
"Now, go show them
what you've got, bae—
that thing that makes
my heart flutter."

Blushing beet red,
I rush up the steps,
grab my accordion,
and join Delgado in front,
a mic stand waiting
for my backup vocals.

Delgado is a natural showman,
kicking up his boots and spinning.
He grabs his mic and tips his hat.
"This first one is for Don Adán.
An oldie but a goodie."

As I pump out the first few notes,
people start to shout and clap,

then the drums and violin join
and we perform "El palomito."

I swear it's like waves of energy
are flowing from the mass
of dancing people, through the air,
and right into my body.

When the crowd joins Delgado and me
for the "currucú, currucú" part,
I forget everything else—
the money, the tragedy, the heartache.

For two and a half minutes,
there's just the musicians
and the music
flowing back and forth
among all these strangers' souls.

JOANNA'S SONG

The song ends, and my head clears.
Joanna made this magic happen,
a gift to me and los Bobbys,
given freely, unselfishly,
without our asking.

But this benefit is not about me
or my friends. Neither is the song
I have been yearning to sing
during these long months
of uncertain worry.

Now I lean forward,
finding her dark eyes
flashing from the front row.
The mic is a magic staff
that will bring the melody
of our first kiss
to vibrant life.

"Esta es para Joanna,
la mera fregona,
Don Adán's beautiful daughter."
Turning to the Bobbys,
I shout, "Let's go, boys!
¡Vámonos recio!"

Bobby Lee hits a key on his laptop,
and synth sounds begin to bounce.
Handy starts his rhythm, waltzy funk,

then accordion and violin launch
into our unique Technojano sound.

I strain to harmonize with Delgado
for the last lines of the chorus:
"Yo no escogí a la Fregona.
¡Ella me escogió a mi!"

The applause as we leave the stage
is wonderful—but more magical
is the kiss that's waiting for me
when Joanna pulls me
behind the speakers.

MEETING MY IDOL

Five other groups perform their sets,
mixes of original songs and favorites
selected by Mr. Padilla.

Then, as the sun sets,
Veronique Medrano takes the stage,
the dazzling light show complementing
her colorful hair, which she tosses with joy,
the unparalleled cool of her outfits,
and her unrivaled voice.

I watch her sing the songs I love—
"Aguas frescas," "Lotería,"
"Tamale Man," and
"Te entrego mi corazón."

I can barely believe my luck.
Joanna leans close, taps my jaw
as if to close my gaping mouth.
"Qué bueno que estás feliz,
but let's not overdo it, yeah?"

Interspersed throughout
come masterful covers
of Tejano greats, like
"Amor prohibido,"
"Bidi Bidi Bom Bom,"
"Si quieres verme llorar,"
and "Hey, Boy."

Veronique wraps up the benefit
with the Freddy Fender hit
"Wasted Days and Wasted Nights,"
and the audience loses its mind!

As older couples clutch and sway
to the old-school tunes,
I grab Joanna and spin her
into the crowd with me.

It's our first slow dance,
and I can't tell whether
the racing heart I feel
is hers or mine.

Afterward, Joanna drags me
backstage to meet my idol.
I'm so nervous, I stutter a hello.

"It's amazing what y'all have done
to bring this community together,
by the way," Verónica says. "Don Adán
must be really proud of his daughter.
And the two of you? Adorable.
Cutest couple I've seen in years."

When all is said and done,
the benefit is a huge success.
We raise ten thousand dollars
that will cover legal costs
and keep the Padillas afloat.

And we raise
people's consciousness
about the issue.

Everything feels like it's shifting,
like we're going to win,
like Mr. Padilla
will soon be
free.

SPOILER ALERT

Things
are not
going
to get
better.

LAI OF RESISTANCE

Time to take a stand.
Such a simple plan:
PERSIST!
We must all demand
our rights in this land:
INSIST!
Do you understand?
Power's in our hands!
RESIST!

THE DECISION

November 15. The immigration judge
lists the evidence against Adán Padilla,
an "undocumented individual
living in the US illegally for two decades."

- speeding
- evading police
- failing to appear in court
- ignoring an arrest warrant
- evading income tax for twenty years

The last item is the final straw.
The government has calculated
Mr. Padilla defrauded them of more
than fifteen thousand dollars
during his time as a self-employed
mechanic. Money is everything.

The judge lifts the stay,
ordering Don Adán
to be immediately
deported.

JUST HOLD ME, GÜERO

A KYRIELLE ADAPTED FROM HER WORDS

Your family is so kind to come
and watch the kids, console my mom.
Let's go outside. I'm feeling weak.
Just hold me, Güero. Let me weep.

They say it's dark before the dawn,
but what if every light is gone?
I pray there's comfort in your heat.
Just hold me, Güero. Let me weep.

I've said a prayer to God above.
Perhaps His answer is your love.
Swear right now you'll never leave.
Just hold me, Güero. Let me weep.

SECOND COLD FRONT

A HAIKU

Gray clouds wrap the world
like graveclothes, blocking the sun—
even nature mourns.

THE SIGN

I'm walking Joanna home
after school, huddled together
against the crooning, crisp wind.

Hanging from her neighbors' fence,
five feet long and three feet high,
is a sign for a new slate of candidates
for the school board election.

Three men, two in cheap suits
that don't quite fit them—
Fernando Jones, former police chief,
and Evaristo Barrera, Snake's dad.
The men who destroyed Adán Padilla.

For a moment, Joanna just stares
at their huge, smiling faces,
then she drops her backpack
and begins to yank ferociously,
grunts becoming wordless shouts
as she rips the plastic free.

Without explanation, she drags the sign
toward her house. I pick up her bag
and follow, afraid for her but knowing
I should not—must not—interfere.

Under the laminate roof
that once gave her father shade,
she takes out a box knife

and begins slashing at the images,
the names above them,
until only ragged ruins remain.

Her gasping breathing slows
as I wait for her, unmoving.
Her eyes are feverish red
when she looks up at me.

"I told you. They always win."

LIKE GOD PROMISED EVE

her:
The snake
in the Garden
of Eden.

What did God promise,
Güero?

Somebody would
crush
the snake under their heel.

me:
Um, yes, her offspring?

her:
All women
are her daughters.

So,
like God promised Eve—

me:
Joanna. You can't.
The second part
is that the snake
will bruise the offspring's heel.

her:
I've been bruised before.

A WEEK WITHOUT HER

Don Adán is staying with family
just across the endless river.
He misses his wife and kids.
They miss him, too.

So of course Doña Bertha
pulls her kids out of school
for a few extra days
during Thanksgiving break.

They need time together,
time to hug their father,
time to laugh and mourn,
time to heal and plan.

But I can't help feeling
that once Joanna crosses over,
she's never coming back,
a spirit stuck in Mictlan.

I cross myself in horror.
A week without her
is hard enough.

Forever would be hell.

THANKSGIVING CIVIL WAR

Thanksgiving is a favorite holiday
for my family, which gathers each year
at Abuela Mimi's house for dinner—
turkey and the traditional fixings.

But this year, there's a huge battle raging.
Teresa started it by pointing out
the holiday erases the suffering
of Native people—like our ancestors.

Our mom and dad, Mimi and Uncle Joe,
most of our cousins say she has a point
and want to listen to her ideas.
But Grandpa Manuel puts his foot down, firm.

"We should celebrate this country's founding!
It gave us freedom, opportunity,
a home like no other nation could give—
and let's face it: The Natives weren't peaceful!"

"I'm not saying the US is all bad.
But Europeans invaded these lands,
sovereign nations with governments and laws,
slaughtered folks, forced women to have their kids."

I chime in to support my big sister.
"That's where our people come from: violent blends.

Can't whitewash the past like nothing happened.
Must respect Native people and ourselves."

A week of arguments and explaining,
then Grandpa Manuel finally relents
when Mimi tells her ex-husband: "My house,
my rules. We're going to follow Teresa."

The gruff Vietnam vet raises his hands.
"Okay. Do we cancel Thanksgiving, then?"
Teresa shakes her head. "No, sir. No need.
We decolonize it, top to bottom."

The first step is the food. Less to change there.
Most is native to the Americas,
but we kids find great recipes online
that use the favorites of our ancestors.

On Thanksgiving Day, everyone arrives
with loads of delicious-smelling dishes.
Mimi pulls the turkey from the oven,
and we sit at the tables she's set up.

Uncle Joe starts to speak. "This land we use
is Comecrudo territory, y'all.
In their language, el río by my ranch
is Atmahau' Pakma't—the Big River.

"We honor them today, their ongoing fight
against the border wall that harms their home,
that destroys the natural habitat
of deer and ocelot and gray wolf."

Teresa teaches us how to say *thanks*
in Nahuatl, an Indigenous tongue
spoken by some of our ancestors—
"Tlazohcamati," we repeat, smiling.

As my dad carves the turkey, we take turns
thanking one another and God as well
for the joy and love we've all received
during a year of hardship and darkness.

Then we dig in! Corn and squash and beans,
sweet potato casserole, tortillas,
and Mimi's great pasilla-rubbed turkey
stuffed with cranberries, plums, and pecans!

Dessert is pumpkin and pecan pie,
crusts made from mesquite and amaranth flour,
sweetened with honey and maple syrup.
I serve myself several hefty slices!

By nightfall, everyone's praising Teresa
for taking a stand and making us wiser,
more responsible, less erasing of the past.
Decolonized Thanksgiving is here to stay!

DOUBTING JOANNA

After a week of no cell service,
Joanna doesn't answer my calls
Saturday or Sunday, either.
She just texts me:
Hablamos el lunes
perdon, wero

Something feels off.
I keep thinking of the sign,
her Old Testament wrath.
So I add las Morras
to a group chat.

Hey, if there's something
going on with la Fregona,
y'all need to tell me.

They all read the message,
but no one responds
until Dalilah finally
sends an audio recording.

"Güero, nothing's going on,
but even if there was,
we don't *need* to tell you
a freaking thing."

Sleep doesn't come easy.
I toss and turn between
nightmares in which

Joanna lies bruised
and bleeding.

Then
at 5:00 a.m.
my phone
chimes.

It's Lupe Paz.
They've left
a message.

"I wouldn't normally rat out a friend,
but I'm frankly scared out of my mind.
Joanna plans to get to school early
and lure Narciso Barrera from practice
to a place with security cameras.
The girls will be there with phones, too.
Then she's going to taunt that moron
until he attacks her, just so she can
get him expelled. Stop her, please."

No. No. No. No.

My heart feels like
a monster just sat on my chest,
squeezing my breath and blood away
before it devours me whole.

I throw my blanket off
and rush to the bathroom.

Five minutes later,
I'm out the front door.

CONFRONTATION

I sprint to the school,
head toward the practice field.
Snake isn't there.

"He's with your girlfriend,
by the portables,"
a linebacker snarls.
"Guess she needed a real man."

Racing across the turf,
ignoring their jeers,
I come to a lit graveled area
between two makeshift classrooms.

Joanna is standing before Snake,
speaking with quiet fury.
The veins in the quarterback's neck
are standing out like steel cords
that are about to snap,
sending him flying.

"Looks like I hurt your pride, but . . .
¿de qué tienes tanto pinche orgullo?"
Joanna demands. "Of your coke-sniffing,
gambling dad? Of your lonely mom,
que sale de la casa de un pelado diferente
every Saturday morning?"

It's too much. She's gone too far.
Snarling, Snakes pulls back his arm,
big hand balled into a fist as he screams,
"¡Pinche mojada! ¡Ahora vas a ver!"

TAKE THE BLOWS

I tried everything,
only to learn that
I can do nothing
for her.

       But she
has been beaten
enough. At the
very least, I can

take
these
blows
for her.

INTO THE GAP

She is not expecting me
to show up, much less
thrust my scrawny body
into the gap between
Snake and her. My arms
reach back, grab hers,
push her away as gently
as I can before Snake's fist

smashes
into my
face.

      I
crumple,
and he
falls on
me.

      After
the third
blow, I
no longer
feel any-
thing.

Dawning
skies go
black.

IN THE HOSPITAL

I emerge, rising slow,
from the comforting depths
of dreamless, medicated sleep
to find my mother and Joanna
by my side in a hospital room.

"Ay, Dios mío, m'ijo,
I was so worried!
How do you feel?"
She looks me over
and kisses my cheeks.

"Okay? A little groggy.
Ouch. My jaw is sore."

"A poco." Mom seems mad.
"That huerco desgraciado
punched you a bunch of times,
Joanna says. Let me get the doctor."

After she leaves,
Joanna takes my hand.
"Why, Güero?"

"I should be asking you
the same question.
Why, Joanna? I mean,
I know why you set him up,
but why not tell me?
Why put yourself at risk?"

She kisses my fingers.
"It's who I am. You know that.
We failed to stop the deportation,
so I figured I'd make Snake pay.
But I couldn't ask anyone else
to be his target. I had to be tough."

I touch her cheek gently.
"That's not tough. That's lonely.
And you are not alone.
I'm with you. I'm no fighter,
but I'll never let anyone hurt
or disrespect you, Joanna.
I will put myself between you
and them every time."

Sniffling, she rubs at her eyes
and grins despite the hitch
of a sob in her chest.

"That's beautiful, Güero.
But aren't you curious?"

I cock my head to one side,
then wince at the soreness.

"Curious about what?"

She stamps her heel
on the floor with a bang.

"What happened to Snake."

WHAT HAPPENED TO SNAKE

ADAPTED FROM JOANNA'S WORDS

When Snake started punching you,
Dalilah and Samantha came running
from where they'd been hiding,
recording with their phones.

They pulled me away, screaming
and kicking, because I was ready
to romperle la madre a ese vato,
but they knew that, ni modo,
the plan was already in motion.

Lucky for us, Victoria had found
a security guard, and he showed up
just in time to stop Snake from beating
you even worse. Lupe had called
911, so both the district cops and
an ambulance were on the scene quick.

Long story short?
He's been expelled.
Off the team,
to the alternative campus,
out of our lives.

Of course, they also suspended *me*,
because I "incited violence
on school property."

Still, that's how it goes, ¿que no?
The victim must be punished, too.
Our great system demands it.

But, hey, at least this way
I get to stay by your side
till you recover.

Did you know you snore?

THE LULL

Life comes in cycles—
the wild adrenaline rush
followed by the lull.

We spend weeks in peace,
recovering, body and soul,
savoring the calm.

Gnawing at me in the silence
is the certainty of change.

DELGADO LEAVES THE BAND

A SEDŌKA, BROKEN

Delgado:
Won't be at practice
have to leave the band, sorry
need time to deal with some stuff

me:
Wait, what do you mean?
we can help with whatever. . . .
we're your brothers, man!

Delgado:
                        Sorry

MOVING TO MEXICO

A knock at our front door.
It's Joanna, sobbing.
Mom leads her in,
sits her down, hugs her,
while I crouch
and take her hands.

At last she can speak.
"Apá found us a house.
Across the river. In Mexico.
Too expensive to keep
the family split up.
Hard on their marriage,
and Amá is worried
that her resident card
will get revoked anyway.
So we're . . . We're moving.
Moving to Mexico.
Leaving the US."

The news is a gut punch.
I drop backward onto the tile.
Dad has just walked in.
Mom explains the situation.

"No," I whisper, crying.
"That's not fair.
What about school?
If you move,

we'll hardly see
each other."

Joanna moans,
reaches for me,
and soon we're
weeping together
while my parents
try to calm us down.

"You don't have to
leave school," Dad says.
"Deja hablo con tu amá.
Güero and I could pick you up
every morning at the bridge,
then drop you off after school."
"Really?" Joanna asks,
her face brightening
as she wipes away tears.

"Pos claro. Your parents
could drop you off and
pick you up at the bridge
on the other side.
It's a short walk."

We take Joanna home.
Mrs. Benavides agrees.

What a relief! It'll be tough,
but she'll still be
with her friends
and with me.

HOLDING HANDS
IN DAD'S OLD TRUCK

A TROVA

Twice a day forget the world—
fifteen minutes of pure luck.
All things fade except my girl—
holding hands in Dad's old truck.

WEEKEND TOGETHER

Mom's brother Santiago
has moved from Monterrey.
He got a management job
in a maquiladora right over
the bridge. I convince Mom
to let me stay with Tío Chago
one weekend so I can spend
more time with Joanna.

Saturday morning we walk
through the town plaza,
hand in hand, watching
pingos play with balloons
as mariachis wander
among the tourists.

We order huge hamburgers,
Mexican style, with egg
and avocado and asadero
cheese dripping everywhere.

Then we catch an afternoon
lucha match between her hero,
el Dandy Junior, and the crude
monster-masked rudo el Cucu.

After a merienda of elote en vaso,
I walk her back to her new home,
where the twins insist that I play
hide-and-seek for an hour with them.

Tío Chago picks me up near dusk,
and we have dinner, catching up.

I fall asleep on his couch while
on the phone with Joanna (neither
of us ever wants to hang up now).
When the sun is up, I shower
and dress for church, accompanying
the Padillas to their new parish,
San Martín de Porres.

Mass. Lunch. Chatting about music
with Don Adán. Then Joanna takes
me for a slow walk in the shade
of mesquites beside an oxbow lake.
We find ourselves a new tree—
I shield her from a December breeze
and kiss her softly before I must go,
making new memories.

BOBBY LEE
CONFIDES IN ME

After school, Bobby Lee
walks with me. Handy's sick,
and God knows what's up
with Delgado.

"I think I scared him away,"
Lee finally says, voice raspy
with sadness. "I've wanted
to tell you, but the time
wasn't right."

"How? What could you do
that would scare that dude
from anything
he wants to do?"

Bobby Lee stops
in the middle of the orchard
where I kissed Joanna
for the first time.

His eyes are red.
His hands are shaking.
"I told him something."

Narrowing my eyes,
I turn to face him.

"What? Why are you
so nervous, carnal?"

"I've got a crush . . .
someone in our grade . . .
a guy we hang out with.
That's what I told Delgado.
He totally freaked out.
Misunderstood everything."

Wheels turn in my head.
Things make sudden sense.

"You told him first.
Before anyone, right?"

"He's been my best friend
since second grade, man.
Of course I told him first.
But now he thinks *he's* the guy
that I'm into."

"He's not?"

"No," he says, looking away,
then staring at his shoes.
"I like someone else."

A pause as I consider
the implications
of his downcast eyes.

"Pues, let me talk
to that moron, then.

As for the rest—
kórale, wey.
If you need advice,
I managed to get
the toughest girl
at school
to fall for me."

He can't help but giggle,
his shoulders shuddering,
as he responds in our private
Hanmegsiko slang.

"Aishiwawa, chinguate!
I forgot you were such
a Romeo. Aiguramba!"

We bump
our fists
and laugh
till we
cry.

GHAZAL FOR GUADALUPE TONANTZÍN

WRITTEN DECEMBER 12

Atop a hill that was normally bare, rose-
bushes bloomed. Juan Diego, after prayer, rose

to obey your gentle command. Up the slope
he walked, toward those blossoming fair rows.

You appeared and arranged in his tilma
thorny stems as straight as arrows.

"Remember: I, your mother, am here,"
you said, your voice like the song of sparrows.

And when those flowers spilled out before the bishop,
there was your holy image, which moves even pharaohs.

It's on this candle that I light to guide my heart,
like toward a distant flare a drifting sailor rows.

CONFRONTING BOBBY DELGADO

"The band needs you,"
I tell Bobby Delgado.
We're standing beside
Rosy's Drive-Thru,
eating Takis preparados.

Before he can answer,
I add, "And I know
the real reason you left.
It makes me hate you
a little, dude. Never thought
you had those prejudices."

"I'm not homophobic,"
he insists indignantly.
"But I'm also not gay,
so I wanted to give him
time to get over it."

I shake my head.
"By 'it' you mean
you think he likes
you. But he doesn't."

"Yeah, yeah, whatever.
Then who does he like?"

I let out a deep sigh.
In my mind, Lee's dark
eyes glance my way,
full of stuff I'm only
now understanding.

"I'm pretty sure it's me.

But I decided not to ask."

Delgado stares at me for a while,
lips moving soundlessly
as he grapples
with the revelation.
Then he sighs.
"What are you going to do?"

"Nothing, Delgado.
I have a girlfriend,
and he adores Joanna,
so he'll never mention it.
I'll just pretend I don't know.
So will you. ¿Me captas?
We're friends.
Bandmates.
Carnales.
I'm not letting anyone
or anything
ruin that."

THOSE THREE WORDS

It's the last day of school,
every class a party,
every laugh bittersweet.

I can't let this day end,
not without telling her,
not without saying it.

It's not skipping class
when no one cares,
so I call her out.

We make our way
to the portables
on the north side.

I hold both her hands,
look deep into her eyes,
those bottomless pools.

Before I lose my nerve,
I say those three words.

I say them in every
language I know.

I say them with my full
thirteen-year-old heart.

Words that echo endless
from the lips of the first couple
in that distant garden.

I love you.
Yo te quiero.
Nan neol saranghae.
Nimitztlazohtla.

WINTER BREAK BEGINS

Though it's only three weeks,
though we have smartphones,
though we'll see each other
and talk every day online,
we feel fate gnaw at our hearts
as we stand in the parking lot
beside the international bridge,
ignoring the rattling motor
of my father's old truck
as we take this last look,
exchange a final kiss,
whisper *Goodbye* and
I'll miss you, bae,
fingers slowly
slipping
away.

CHRISTMAS DAY
EPILOGUE

ALL I TRULY WANT

I wake up early, go outside—
our yard still glitters white.
Till the sun climbs high enough to melt
the magic we beheld.

Soon all my family will wake up,
open presents and have fun.
I'll smile at them and laugh along,
maybe sing some Christmas songs.

But they'll slide into minor, like the blues,
for all I truly want to do
is see the girl who rules my heart—
I can't wait for school to start.

GLOSSARY

"Festive Barbecue"
Tíos [TEE-ohs] uncles (or uncles and aunts together)
Primos [PREE-mohs] cousins

"Border Snow"
Güero [WEH-roh] person with pale skin
¡Está nevando! [ehs-TAH neh-BAHN-do] It's snowing!
Te hablo mañana [TEH AH-bloh mahn-YAH-nah] I'll call you tomorrow

"My Journal"
Huercos [WER-kohs] impish little kids

"Los detallitos"
Detallitos [deh-tah-YEE-tohs] small actions or gifts that show your feelings

"Sunday Morning at the Taquería"
Taqueria [tah-keh-REE-ah] restaurant that sells tacos
Fútbol [FOOT-bohl] soccer
Salsa verde [SAL-sah BEHR-theh] green salsa
Buenos días [WEH-nohs THEE-ahs] good morning
¿Qué tal? [KEH TAHL] How's everything going?
¿Y su familia? [EE SOO fah-MEEL-yah] And your family?
En casa [EN KAH-sah] at home
Taquitos [tah-KEE-tohs] breakfast tacos (regionally, on the Texas–Mexico border)
Cosas de adultos [KOH-sahs theh ah-THOOL-tohs] grown-up stuff

M'ijo [MEE-hoh] my son
Almuerzo [al-MWER-soh] hot breakfast

"THE KISS"
Fregona [freh-GO-nah] tough girl

"THEY CALL HER FREGONA"
Lucha libre [LOO-chah LEE-breh] Mexican wrestling
Sartén [sar TEN] skillet
Fregar [freh GAR] to scrub, to annoy, to do hard or tough things
Fresas [FREH-sahs] slang for stuck-up, middle-class, or rich people
Apá [ah-PAH] "pops," shortened form of papá or "father"

"ROMANTIC ADVICE"
Abuela [ah-WEL-ah] grandmother
Bisabuela [bee-sahb-WEL-ah] great-grandmother
Tío [TEE-oh] uncle
Tía [TEE-ah] aunt

"MY OWN RESEARCH"
Telenovelas [teh-leh-noh-BEH-lahs] Latin American soap operas

"HOW MOM AND DAD GOT TOGETHER"
Azotea [ah-soh-TEH-ah] the flat roof of a Mexican home
Caray [kah-RYE] My goodness! Wow!

"GÜERO Y LOS BOBBYS"
El Chaparro [el chah-PAH-roh] shorty
Para que veas [PAH-rah keh BEH-ahs] proof, in case you had any doubts

"First Date"
Las Morras [lahs MOH-rahs] "the Girls" (slang), the name everyone calls Joanna's group of friends
Vamos a comer algo ya let's eat something already
Ay güey [eye WEY] oh crap

"Meeting Her Parents"
¿A qué equipo de fútbol le vas? What soccer team do you root for?
Bueno, ¿qué quieres ser de grande? Okay, what do you want to be when you grow up?
¿No vas a trabajar con tu papá en la construcción? Aren't you going to work with your dad in construction?
¡Pero si gana bien! But he makes good money!
Por supuesto [por soo-PWES-toh] of course

"Joanna and las Morras"
Les Morres [lehs MOH-rehs] a gender-neutral alternative to morros (boys) or morras (girls), like "kids" or "teens," but less common
Eres su primer novio you are her first boyfriend

"Joanna's First Bully"
Chompuda [chohm-POO-thah] with messy hair, all askew
Piojosa [pyoh-HOH-sah] girl with lice
Prieta [PRYEH-tah] girl with very dark skin, used as an insult in this context
Di lo que quieras de mí, baboso say what you want about me, stupid
Pero no vuelvas a mencionar a mi mamá but don't ever mention my mom again

"Two Mother's Days"
El mes de mayo the month of May
Día diez [DEE-ah THYEZ] day ten
Mexicana [meh-hee-KAH-nah] Mexican woman or girl

"Baby Pictures"
Qué chulo [keh CHOO-loh] how cute
¿Verdad? [ber-DAHD] Right?
Un gordito enojón [oon gor-THEE-toh eh-noh-HOHN] an angry little chubby baby
Flaco [FLAH-koh] skinny, often an endearing nickname
Amá [ah-MAH] mom
Apá se mochaba [ah-PAH seh moh-CHAH-bah] dad paid him a bribe
Nomás lo que es just what's fair
Nada que llame la atención Nothing too conspicuous, too obvious

"Ten Things I know about Each of the Bobbys"
Me da flojera [meh thah floh-HEH-rah] I'm too lazy to do it
Santería [sahn-teh-REE-ah] religion that blends African, Indigenous, and Catholic traditions

"Awards Ceremony"
Naca [NAH-kah] low-class, cheap (often used by lighter-skinned Mexican people against darker-complexioned folks)

"The Tornado and My Bedroom"
Tejabán [teh-hah-BAHN] cheaply made wooden house
Pero amá estaba encinta but mom was pregnant

"What the Hallyu?"
Tacos de bistec [TAH-kohs theh bees-TEK] chopped-steak tacos

"Hanmegsiko Slang!"
Órale [OH-dah-leh] cool, sure, you bet
Ay chihuahua [eye chee-WAH-wah] oh gosh, OMG
No manches [noh MAHN-chehs] you've got to be kidding
Lero lero [LEH-roh LEH-roh] a taunting cry that kids use, like "nanny nanny boo boo"

"My Town in June"
La vecina [lah beh-SEE-nah] the neighbor woman
Raspa [RAHS-pah] shaved ice with flavored syrup
Comadres [koh-MAH-drehs] women who are good friends
La Rubia [lah ROO-byah] the blonde girl
El Maistro [el MIGH-stroh] the expert construction worker
Placita [plah-SEE-tah] little plaza

"Beach Barbecue"
Fajitas [fah-HEE-tahs] beef skirt steak
Nopal [noh-PAL] prickly pear cactus
Que cada quien se sirva everybody serves themselves

"Teresa's Announcement"
Latinx [lah-TEEN-eks] a gender-neutral alternative to Latina or Latino

"What's with the X?"
Tejano [teh-HAH-noh] Mexican American man from Texas; also, a style of music
Chicano [chee-KAH-noh] Mexican American (often a progressive person, an activist)
Mexicano [meh-hee-KAH-noh] A Mexican man or boy; also, a Mexican person whose gender isn't specified or known
Latino [lah-TEE-noh] people of Latin American ancestry living in the US
Pos [pohs] filler word like "uh" or well

Gente [HEN-teh] people
Latine [lah-TEE-neh] a gender-neutral way of saying "Latino"

"JUNTOS CON CONJUNTO"
Caliche [kah-LEE-cheh] a light-colored gravel from hot regions
Dime, ingrata [DEE-meh een-GRAH-tah] Tell Me, Ungrateful Girl (title of a song)
Los Alegres de Terán The Happy Ones from Terán (a musical group)
¿Cómo lo sabes? [KOH-moh loh SAH-bes] How do you know that?
Esta camioneta tiene [ES-tah kah-myoh-NEH-tah TYEH-neh] this truck has
Balada [bah-LAH-thah] ballad
Ranchera [rahn-CHEH-dah] a type of song
Conjunto [kohn-HOON-toh] a style of music
Norteño [nor-TEH-nyoh] a style of music
Estos señores [ES-tohs seh-NYOH-des] these gentlemen
Los Gorriones del Topo Chico The Sparrows of Topo Chico (a musical group)
Los Donneños [los dohn-NEH-nyos] The Ones from Donna (a musical group)
No sabía que te gustaba la buena música I didn't know you liked good music
¿Y esto? [ee ES-toh] What's this?
Es el poder del conjunto, m'ija it's the power of the conjunto, my daughter

"LUCHA WITH THE PADILLAS"
Picosos [pee-KOH-sos] spicy
La Momia [la MOH-myah] The Mummy
Trampa [TRAHM-pah] trick
Técnico [TEK-nee-koh] good guy (in wrestling)
Rudo [ROO-thoh] bad guy (in wrestling)

"Mixtape for Don Adán"

Feliz día [feh-LEES THEE-ah] hope you're enjoying your special day

Le traje algo [leh TRAH-heh AL-goh] I brought you something

La Fiebre [la FYEH-breh] The Fever (a band)

A ver si le atiné hopefully I was spot-on [in my choices]

Me trataba bien [meh trah-TAH-bah byen] he treated me well

Decían [deh-SEE-ahn] they said

Pues sí [pwes see] well, yes

Lo feo [lo FEH-oh] the ugly part

Así es [ah-SEE es] that's right

Policía chueco [poh-lee-SEE-ah CHWEH-koh] crooked/corrupt cop

Me bajó una feria he made me give him a bribe

¿Me explico? [me ex-PLEE-koh] Am I clear?

"How Delgado Got His Voice"

Ache [AH-cheh] "ashe," a divine gift (in Santería and other belief systems derived from West African Yoruba religion)

Oricha [oh-REE-chah] "Orisha," an important spirit or deity (in Santería and other belief systems derived from West African Yoruba religion)

"Our Tree"

Bosque [BOS-keh] forest

"La Llorona in the Canal"

La Llorona [lah yoh-ROH-nah] the Wailing Woman

"Fractures at Practice"

Electro-Tejano [eh-LEK-troh teh-HAH-noh] a kind of music that blends electronica and Tejano

"Mr. Padilla Wakes Us Up"
A ver si entiendo let's see if I understand
Tú te quieres imponer you want to impose your opinions
Carnales [kar-NAH-les] bros, brothers, close friends
¿Y bien? ¿Van a tocar o qué? And then? Are y'all going to play or what?

"What Happens to Mr. Padilla"
Papá [pah-PAH] dad
¡Lo agarraron, mamá! Los de ICE They snatched him up, Mom! The guys from ICE

"Snake Bite"
Préstame tu celular [PREHS-tah-meh too sel-loo-LAHR] lend me your cell phone
El Chino [el CHEE-noh] the Chinese kid, used as an insult in this context
El Pocho [el POH-choh] not quite Mexican, not quite American (potentially insulting)
Dominicano [doh-mee-nee-KAH-noh] Dominican
Morenita [moh-reh-NEE-tah] little dark-skinned girl, used as an insult in this context
Hijo de la gran son of a

"Trying to Comfort Joanna"
Güey [wey] dude

"Texting that Night"
La migra [lah MEE-grah] immigration (ICE)
Broncas [BROHN-kahs] beef, problems, trouble

"It's Not Castellano"
Mi llamo [meh YAH-moh] My name is (non-standard Spanish)

Orita yo y mis Right now, me and my (non-standard Spanish)

Y mis papases estamos viviendo and my parents are living (non-standard Spanish)

Anca la güelita pa' que los roofers tengan chance at grandma's place so the roofers have a chance (non-standard Spanish)

De hacer repair el roof de nuestra casa to repair the roof of our house (non-standard Spanish)

Castellano [kahs-teh-YAH-noh] Castilian Spanish (considered "proper" Spanish by many college-educated, middle-class people throughout Latin American and Spain)

A ver, joven, ¿tiene una pregunta? Yes, young man, do you have a question?

No, profesor. Una explicación No, teacher. An explanation

Lo que hablamos aquí no es castellano what we speak here isn't Castilian Spanish

Es español mexicano [es es-pah-NYOL meh-hee-KAH-noh] it's Mexican Spanish

Y mi compañero emplea el dialecto fronterizo and my classmate is employing the border dialect

Que todos los presentes entendemos that all of us here understand

Sin problemas [seen proh-BLEH-mahs] without problems

Usted también [oos-TED tahm-BYEN] including you

me imagino [meh ee-mah-GEE-noh] I'm guessing

"WHAT'S YOUR REAL NAME?"

Chicana [chee-KAH-nah] Mexican American woman / girl (often a progressive person, an activist)

Pero es solo un apodo but it's just a nickname

A nadie le importa tu estúpido nombre no one cares about your stupid name

"Phone Call with Papá"

Acá mis ojos [ah-KAH mees OH-hohs] this one over here
(literally, "my eyes over here")

Sé que le ayudas a tu amá I know you help your mom

Pasa tiempo con tus amigas spend time with your [girl]
friends

Vas a ser una mujer importante you're going to be an
important woman

Está bien, Apá [es-TAH byehn ah-PAH] okay, Dad

Pero cuídese [PEH-doh KWEE-theh-seh] but take care of
yourself

"Las Morras"

Chola [CHOH-lah] a Chicana with an urban aesthetic, look, or
lifestyle

Pozole [poh-SOH-leh] a soup from Mexico with hominy and
pork

"La mecánica y el traidor"

Porque son fregaderas [POR-keh sohn freh-gah-THEH-dahs]
because it's BS

Mis jefes [mees HEH-fehs] my folks (slang for parents)

"A la ru-ru"

A la ru-ru, Mari, a la ru-ru ya it's bedtime, Mari, it's bedtime
again

Duérmete, mi Mari, duérmeteme ya go to sleep, dear Mari,
go to sleep now

Esta niña linda se quiere dormir this sweet girl wants to
sleep

Pero ese sueño no quiere venir but the sleep just won't
come

Esta niña linda que nació de día this sweet girl, born when it
was day

Quiere que la lleven a ver a su tía wants to be taken to see her aunt

Esta niña linda que nació de noche this sweet girl, born when it was night

Quiere que la lleven a pasear en coche wants to be taken for a little drive

"LUCKY TO BE IN ESL"

No manches [no MAHN-chehs] you've got to be kidding

¿Verdad que no? [ber-THAHD keh noh] I'll bet not, right?

¿Cuándo vas a aprender, flaco? When are you going to learn, bae?

Ya sé [yah seh] I already know

Pero bueno [PEH-roh WEH-noh] but okay

Dile al director que te ponga conmigo Tell the principal to put you with me

¿No que no? [noh keh noh] Didn't you say you wouldn't?

"WHAT'S WRONG WITH OUR TOWN?"

Mexicanos [meh-hee-KAH-nohs] Mexicans

Nuestra gente [NWES-trah HEN-teh] our people

Morena [moh-REH-nah] dark-skinned woman or girl

Colonia [koh-LOH-nyah] neighborhood, often a poor one in the US

"ECHOES"

Cumbia [KOOM-byah] a type of song

Mi fantasía [mee fahn-tah-SEE-ah] my fantasy

Tan solo de pensar just by thinking

Que te vuelva a besar that I might kiss you again

Mi corazón nervioso [mee koh-rah-SOHN ner-BYOH-soh] my nervous heart

Está late que late beats like mad

"Luisa's Idea"
¿Cómo va lo de don Adán? How's the situation with Don Adán?
En esta comunidad [en ES-tah koh-moo-nee-THAHD] in this community

"Joanna's Request"
Chaneque [chah-NEH-keh] a sort of forest spirit or elf
Chido, ¿sí? [CHEE-thoh SEE] Cool, right?

"Halloween Obstacle Course"
Pingos [PEEN-gohs] little devils, brats
El Cucuy [el koo-KOO-ee] the Bogeyman
Mano Pachona [MAH-noh pah-CHOH-nah] Monster Claw (literally, "hairy hand")

"Día de Muertos"
Papel picado [pah-PEL pee-KAH-thoh] multicolored paper with designs cut in
Mira nuestra familia [MEE-dah NWES-trah fah-MEE-lyah] look at our family

"The Paradox of the Stage"
Demos la bienvenida [DEH-mohs lah byen-beh-NEE-thah] let's all welcome
El palomito [el pah-loh-MEE-toh] The Little Dove (title of a song)
Currucú [koo-roo-KOO] coo, coo (sound doves make)

"Joanna's Song"
Esta es para Joanna, la mera fregona this is for Joanna, the toughest of all

¡Vámonos recio! [BAH-moh-nohs REH-syoh] Let's do this! Kick it!

Technojano [tek-noh-HAH-noh] a blend of *techno* and *Tejano*

Yo no escogí a la Fregona I didn't choose the tough girl

¡Ella me escogió a mí! She's the one who chose me!

"Meeting My Idol"

Aguas frescas [AH-wahs FRES-kahs] drinks made with fresh fruits, flowers, or other plants

Lotería [loh-teh-REE-ah] lottery, a popular board game from Mexico

Te entrego mi corazón I Give You My Heart (title of a song)

Qué bueno que estás feliz how great that you're happy

Amor prohibido [ah-MOHR proh-ee-BEE-thoh] Forbidden Love (title of a song)

Si quieres verme llorar If You Want to See Me Cry (title of a song)

"Thanksgiving Civil War"

Comecrudo [koh-meh-KROO-thoh] an Indigenous nation that lives in deep South Texas

El Río [el REE-oh] the river

Pasilla [pah-SEE-yah] a type of pepper

"Doubting Joanna"

Hablamos el lunes [ah-BLAH-mohs el LOO-nes] we'll talk on Monday

Perdon, wero [per-THOHN WEH-doh] sorry, Güero

"Confrontation"

¿De qué tienes tanto pinche orgullo? What are you so damn proud of?

Que sale de la casa de un pelado diferente who comes out of the house of a different dude
¡Pinche mojada! [PEEN-cheh moh-HAH-thah] Damn wetback! (very offensive slur)
¡Ahora vas a ver! I'll show you!

"IN THE HOSPITAL"
Ay, Dios mío, m'ijo oh, my God, son
A poco [ah POH-koh] Oh really
Huerco desgraciado [WER-koh des-grah-SYAH-thoh] Worthless brat

"WHAT HAPPENED TO SNAKE"
Romperle la madre a ese vato smash that dude's damn face in (offensive)
Ni modo [nee MOH-thoh] too bad
¿Que no? [keh noh] Isn't that right?

"MOVING TO MEXICO"
Deja hablo con tu amá let me talk to your mom
Pos claro [pohs KLAH-roh] well, of course

"WEEKEND TOGETHER"
Maquiladora [mah-kee-lah-DOH-rah] a type of factory
Mariachis [mah-RYAH-chees] a type of traditional Mexican musicians
Merienda [meh-RYEHN-dah] snack
Elote en vaso [eh-LOH-the en BAH-soh] steamed corn in a cup with cream, hot sauce, and mayonnaise

"BOBBY LEE CONFIDES IN ME"
Pues [pwehs] well . . .
Kórale, wey [KOH-rah-leh wey] you got it, dude (blend of Korean and Spanish)

"Confronting Bobby Delgado"
Takis preparados [TAH-kees preh-pah-RAH-thohs] a spicy snack
¿Me captaste? [meh kahp-TAHS-teh] You feel me? You understand?

"Those Three Words"
Yo te quiero [yoh teh KYEH-doh] I love you

This book wouldn't exist without the support and belief of many people. First, a huge thanks to all those who helped make *They Call Me Güero* a reality. Janet Wong and Sylvia Vardell, for commissioning the poem "Border Kid," which launched the whole project. Bobby Byrd for recognizing the promise of that piece and shepherding the original manuscript with a poet's eye. Zeke Peña for the cover illustration that serves as readers' first peek into Güero's border community. The multiple committees across the globe that saw in that first slender volume a timeless story worthy of critical recognition.

But most important, you. The reader. You spent seventh grade with Güero, walked with him down those crowded hallways, ate snacks with him, listened to music alongside him and his great-grandmother, watched him fall in love. And you recognized yourself in him, no matter the difference in region or language or ethnicity. Thank you for making *They Call Me Güero* a success . . . and then demanding more.

In December 2018, before the awards started racking up, I visited Pete Gallegos Elementary School in Eagle Pass, on the Texas-Mexico border. The students put on an amazing show, acting out some of the poems, dancing and singing to my words—which they had set to music with their teachers—in front of a life-size 3-D version of the book's cover. I was completely floored by the reception, by the excitement of the kids, by their willingness to engage with my story on so many levels.

After my presentation, I was approached by a group of young ladies who had been deeply involved in the dramatization of key passages. They wanted to tell me how much they loved the character of Joanna Padilla, "la Fregona," who becomes Güero's girlfriend after rescuing him from a bully.

"She's the best character in the book," they told me. "But she's not in many of the poems. Are you writing a sequel?"

To be honest, the book had just come out. I didn't even know if it was going to be a success. But there was definitely more to tell, more parts of that borderland world to explore.

"Maybe," I told them. "Yeah, I think so."

"Good," the girls said. "Because we want a part two. But it needs to be about Joanna. We need to know her story, too. Please write it."

I promised them that I wouldn't let them down. And in school after school over the next few years, kids of all types asked for the same thing.

Another book. Focused on Joanna la Fregona.

Because, all of them said, her story deserved to be told.

They weren't wrong.

So, knowing that an author must always put the reader first, I began to sketch out the first few poems of the book you now hold in your hands.

For the writing of *They Call Her Fregona*, I owe a *huge* debt of gratitude to my agents, Taylor Martindale Kean and Stefanie von Borstel, who found a great new home for *Güero* and *Fregona* at Penguin Random House. The whole team at its Kokila imprint have been *amazing*, especially my editor, Joanna Cárdenas, who truly and deeply understands Mexican American communities on the border as well as what makes narratives flow and poetry sing. I couldn't have asked for a better partner on this journey. Several friends helped me make sure my depiction of Korean Americans in Güero's community was as authentic as possible: Linda Sue Park, who read a draft and gave me wonderful feedback, as well as Ellen Oh, Jung Kim, and Hanna Kim, who answered all of my questions so patiently.

There have been many fregonas in my life—tías and abuelas, nieces and sisters-in-law, daughters and colleagues. Their strength and resilience, wrapped around a compassionate and sensitive core, have protected and inspired me time and time again over the years. I can only hope that a fraction of their humanity and dignity comes across in these pages. I'm a better person with them as my friends and mentors.

Among them all, I must single out one as the most supportive and influential: my wife, Angélica, la mera fregona de mi alma, without whom nothing I've done would be possible or even worthwhile.

Gracias, amor. Nos vemos pronto bajo nuestro árbol.

—David Bowles
February 20, 2022